BATTLE FOR EARTH

The Vaedra Chronicles Series Book 5

ESTER LÓPEZ

ESTER'S READERS GROUP

www.esterlopez.com

THE WHITE HOUSE

After landing on the lawn of the leader's home, Chief Medical Officer Conn grabbed her Med bag and left the Concordance's transporter.

She had examined the reptilian's blood sample and was able to create a test to determine if someone was human or reptilian. The thought that a reptilian had been a passenger on the Concordance gave her pause. *This cannot happen again. The Admiral must take precautions in letting people board the star destroyer.*

She followed the security contingency, along with CMOs Shim and Torres, to a small group of armed guards waiting for them.

"We're here to meet with your leader," Denton, Conn's head of security, said.

"Is this everyone?" the armed guard asked.

"Yes."

"I'm Hastings. Follow me." Hastings turned and they followed along behind him. The small group rounded the tall, white building and entered through the front door. Once inside, a man whose name badge said Smith asked the Concordance Security to relinquish their weapons.

"We will keep our weapons," Denton said.

"I'm sorry, but you can't go any farther with your weapons," Smith said. Hastings stood beside Smith and pressed his ear, speaking softly.

Conn moved forward in the group. "Excuse me, but we have urgent information for your leader. Our Security will need their weapons for the protocols we are to put in place."

Smith stared at her and pulled his weapon. She heard movement from her own security behind her.

"Like I said, you can't go any farther with your weapons."

The Concordance Security had drawn their weapons at the same time.

"We are at a standoff, and this is urgent. Have your leader come to us," she said.

Hastings tapped Smith's shoulder. "Gowan wants to speak to you." Hastings handed a small device to Smith, and he listened. Then he put his weapon up and ushered them inside. Hastings left the group.

Smith ushered them through a door off to the side of the entrance way.

"Mr. President, I'm Chief Medical Officer Conn from the Concordance, and these are my counterparts, CMO Shim from the Reliance and CMO Torres from the Endeavor." She shook the outstretched hand of the President and watched as the others did the same.

"We are also healers," she said.

"Have a seat," the President said. He gestured to the chairs in the room.

She bowed and sat down. "The three of us have been

working in our labs, creating the blood test that will show you who is human and who is not."

"We have blood tests here as well," the President said.

"Yes, but I assure you, this test will let you know immediately so you can take swift action."

"What do you mean by that?"

"The Draco Reptilians won't stand still for this. They will fight or run. If they refuse the test, we have our security force who will stun them temporarily so they can be tested. If they are not human, you must decide whether to destroy them or hold them prisoners."

"Do you think it's that serious? I knew we had reptilians on this planet working with the cabal, but I never thought we had them here in the White House," the President said.

"Yes sir. It is," CMO Torres said. "The Draco Reptilians embed themselves into government agencies where they take over that government."

"They gain control of the planets from within, by shapeshifting into humans," Conn said.

"Have you had recent turmoil and violence in your part of your world?" CMO Shim asked.

"Yes actually. It's been happening all over the planet, especially after UFO sightings," the President said.

"UFO sightings?" Conn asked.

"Unidentified flying objects. You know, alien space craft," the President said.

"It is worse than I thought," Conn said. She glanced at her counterparts. There wasn't much time to check everyone, but they had to start somewhere, and it had to be now.

"Do you have labs that can duplicate our blood tests?" CMO Torres asked.

"Yes, we do, but not here. We would have to go off the premises."

"We need to test everyone at the lab first to avoid sabotage. We also need to test everyone in your government," Conn said.

"Everyone?"

"Yes sir. Otherwise, you won't know whom to trust," CMO Torres said.

"I can have all the staff come to one of our meeting rooms. Will that work?"

"It should be fine. Are there any others who work in this building besides the staff?"

"I have the Secret Service and the Military that are stationed here. Then there are the service people like the chef and his assistants, as well as a few others. Did you need to test them as well?"

"We should test everyone, just to be safe," Conn said. She glanced at CMO Torres. "Maybe we should split up and one of us stay here while the other two go to the lab and get started?" she said.

"We'll go to the lab," CMO Shim said, pointing to Torres and himself.

The President whispered to his security officer and the officer spoke into his device.

"I'll have the Secret Service drive you to the lab," the President said. "They will bring you back when you're finished. How long do you think it will take?"

"Thank you, sir. It could take hours for us to duplicate the tests and then test the individuals there," CMO Torres said.

"How many people do you think are there at the lab?" CMO Shim asked.

"That, I don't know. Why do you have to test the people at the lab?"

"To make sure there is no sabotage of the test kits. If there are Dracos present, they will try to stop us because they know we will know who they are," CMO Shim said.

Within minutes, a Secret Service agent arrived.

"You two *do* have your comm links with you?" Conn asked.

"Yes," Shim raised his arm, exposing his wrist comm.

"Right here," Torres pointed to his shoulder comm.

She checked her wrist as well to make sure hers was on.

The Secret Service Agent escorted CMOs Shim and Torres out the door. Four of the six security guards left with them.

"Come this way," the President said. He showed her to a large meeting room. She was followed by Denton and the last of their security guards, Tars.

"While you are setting up, I'll get my staff here." The President left with his Secret Service Agents.

Conn set her Med bag on a table across from the door. To her far right was a large oval table surrounded by many chairs. It must be where the President had his meetings. She proceeded to take out the small devices for checking blood, as well as the testing strips. She then popped open a small container to hold the discarded items.

"If one of you can line them up, I'll do the test and check it, while the other watches for reactions. It should take a minute per person."

"What kind of reactions are you looking for?" Tars asked.

"If they refuse, use half stun on them," Denton said.

"Any other reactions?" Tars asked.

"Well, if they turn into a reptile, hit them twice on full stun," Conn said.

~

CMO Shim and CMO Torres, along with their four security guards, loaded into a large limousine, sitting three to a seat, facing each other. They made small talk for a while when Shim realized the ride seemed to take a long time before they came to a stop at a tall building. The driver remained in his seat on the other side of a glass partition. Someone at the front door of the building came toward them. He opened their door, leaned in a little, and pressed a small device in his hand, aimed inside the vehicle.

"Follow me," he said.

Shim got out first, then a guard, then Torres, and the other three guards.

"Hey, my stunner isn't working," the first guard said.

Everyone stopped. The other three guards checked their stunners.

"Mine's dead too."

Shim tapped his comm link. "My comms are down."

Two of the guards pounded their weapons, but they were all useless.

Shim watched as the driver pulled away.

"Was he supposed to wait on us?" Shim asked.

The man who led them out of the vehicle didn't answer. Instead, he turned and walked away from the group.

That's odd behavior, Shim thought.

Torres tried his comm link, with no luck.

"What's going on here?" Torres asked.

The man who led them turned back around, a weapon in his hand. He pointed the weapon at all of them.

The Concordance, Above Earth's Moon

Adam Davis paced back and forth in the small quarters he

shared with his mate, Genesis. He had wanted his new friends to share their technology with Earth, but instead, found the Earth in turmoil. Grey aliens had tried to take out the power grids with EMF weapons, but the Star Forces from the Concordance, the Reliance, and the Endeavor had managed to stop them.

They had just returned on their first diplomatic mission to show the Earthens how things were done in the Vaedra system. Then they found out one of the passengers on the Concordance, an NSA employee, was not even human when he tried to kill Torren Conley on the Moon.

"I can't stand by and do nothing." He ran a hand through his hair. "That's my planet over there, my home. I'm the one who brought all these people together."

"My home is with you. But you didn't start the trouble that is on your planet." Genesis stood and touched his arm. He stopped pacing.

"Whatever you decide, Adam, I am with you."

"Let's go find Tremol and see what we can do," he said. He put his arm around her and gave her a hug. She squeezed him back and they headed down the hall to the people mover.

Captain Tremol and his mate, Keely, sat across from Captain Gadara and her mate, Torren Conley, in the Officers Lounge on Deck One, when Adam and Genesis entered the Lounge. Keely waved them over. Adam sat next to Torren and Genesis sat across from him, next to Keely.

"When do you start your new assignment?" Keely asked Captain Gadara.

"We start tomorrow," she said.

Adam glimpsed Gadara reaching to Torren's thigh and giving it a squeeze. Torren turned toward her. "They are sending us to Edwards Air Force Base," Torren said, glancing at all of them.

"Edwards? Isn't that where they keep alien ships?" Keely asked.

"Yes, we will be training for two months before they send us to the moons of Mars," Gadara said. She smiled at Torren.

"What will you be doing on the moons of Mars?" Adam asked.

"I think we will be working on building a base there," Torren said.

"Whatever for? Is there any kind of precious metal there?" Adam asked.

"I guess we will find out when we go through training," Gadara said.

"What about you two?" Keely glanced at Genesis and then Adam.

"That's why we are here," Genesis said.

The barkeep brought some drinks for Tremol, Keely, Gadara, and Torren. "What are you two drinking?" The barkeep looked at Adam.

"Two ales, please."

When the barkeep left, he spoke up, glancing at Tremol. "What's the word on Earth?"

"Conn and the other Chief Medical Officers from the Reliance and Endeavor left with their security for the White House." Tremol said.

"They are initiating the testing," Keely added. "We were told to wait here for further instructions."

"What about all the dignitaries?"

"After they were all tested here, Keely and I flew them to

the White House with our security. They are in a bunker for debriefing, waiting for clearance." Tremol said.

"Genesis and I want to help. What can we do?" he asked.

The barkeep returned with their drinks. Before leaving, the barkeep glanced over Adam's head to the entrance. Adam turned around to see Admiral Esrith walk in with his son Eno and two others.

2

THE WHITE HOUSE

Denton kept the line outside the room so Tars would deal with only one person at a time. Tars is their newest security recruit and it was up to Denton to train him.

Conn worked quickly and had determined the first three people were human when a Secret Service agent ushered everyone inside the room, disrupting her activities. The large table on the far side of the room forced everyone to line up around the table. She glanced at Denton to get an explanation for the change in plans when she noticed the agent's weapon was up under Denton's chin.

"What's the meaning of this?" she demanded. She was furious. Were the President's people that inept that they couldn't follow orders?

"The meaning?" The agent shook violently, turning into a seven-foot brownish-green reptile. His clothes ripped apart in his transition. Damn reptilian. This is not how she envisioned their first encounter. The situation was out of control.

Denton worked quickly, pulling his stunner he fired at the creature. It took two shots, but the creature fell over.

Everyone gasped and huddled on the far side of the room. The staff was evenly divided between men and women. Tars was at the end of the clustered group, closer to her. She watched him pull his stunner out.

"Anyone else have a secret they want to share?" Tars called out as he waved his stunner at the group. The group spread out immediately.

Before she could think, four Secret Service agents shoved the door open, barging into the room. They knocked Denton off balance. The last one in slammed the door shut and locked it. Denton took a shot at him with the stunner, but got only one shot off before another agent hit Denton with his weapon. The loud pop made her jump. At least the Vaedran weapons were quiet. Denton lay on the ground, bleeding. Was he dead? She was unfamiliar with Earth weapons.

The agent that Denton shot at the door fell, shifting into a large reptile. His clothes were also ripped apart. The first of the remaining agents shot out the cameras in the room. Some of the female staff screamed at the chaos.

Tars took a shot at the agent shooting out the cameras, but was also shot by another agent. The one Tars shot fell to the ground and shifted as well.

They were down to two agents, now, most likely reptilians as well. Conn stood paralyzed. She needed to check on Denton and Tars. If she went to check on either guard, would they shoot her as well? If all five of these agents were reptilian, and they worked for the President, did he realize how compromised his team was?

She glanced at Tars, then spoke to the two agents who were remaining. "I'm a healer. Can I please check him?" She pointed to Tars.

"No. There will be no healing today."

The staff had crowded closer together. Some of them

were sobbing. She had to warn them. These creatures fed off fear.

The two creatures who were recently stunned would be out for only fifteen minutes. The first one that Denton stunned twice would be out for hours.

"Get over there." The agent motioned with his weapon. He pointed to the opposite side of the table from where Tars lay. As she walked to that side of the room, she fidgeted with her comm link on her wrist. If she could punch the right button, it would send a distress signal and the security on the Concordance could find her. She twisted the comm just right, turning it on the side of her wrist. She played with her hair, turning her body to make it easier to catch a vid-feed of what was going on. She only hoped the creatures wouldn't catch on to her movements.

Now, if she could get one of the stunners, she would be able to knock out another guard. Then what? They would shoot her dead, too. But the agents didn't seem to make a move to retrieve them. She would have to try again later. As she joined the group, the two agents shuddered violently and turned into the reptilians they were.

"Shhh. You must remain calm. They feed off your fear," she whispered.

"Calm?" a man replied in a whisper. "How can we remain calm after seeing that?"

"Exactly," one of the reptilians replied. "I can smell your fear and it's making me hungry." He jumped onto the table.

The small group, including her, jerked at the movement of the creature on the table. These reptilians were more intimidating hovering over them so closely.

The other reptilian joined him on the table. "What did they hit our friends with?" He looked right at her.

"It was a stun weapon. They are not dead, only stunned," she replied. Now she wished they *were* dead. How were they going to escape this mess?

"For how long?"

"Several minutes to several hours depending on how many times they were hit." She hoped that answer would appease them.

"Looks like we will be here for a while," the first one said.

The Reliance, Above Earth's Atmosphere

The Joint Chiefs of Staff, along with the Pleiadians, Vaedrans, Arcturans, Orions, and some other races from the Galactic Federation, met in Admiral Tibbets' map room. It was quite crowded, with standing room only. Esrith removed his hat and ran his hand through his hair.

"Admiral Tibbets," General Thompson of the U.S. Army began, "the White Hats of the U.S. Military have been in control of addressing the sex trafficking of children in the United States. We have been working with White Hats of other nations as well and have just about completed our work, rescuing the children and adults who have been trafficked around the world. We have systematically destroyed all the tunnels and deep underground military bases used by these traffickers and the reptilians working with them. We need help in stopping and capturing the greys and reptilians who are trying to escape Earth."

"May I speak?" a tall blond man asked of Admiral Tibbets. Tibbets nodded.

The man stood and addressed the group. "I am Kalig from the Pleiades. The Grand Spiritual Council of Light was forged long ago. We are composed of many races committed to helping Earth ascend. We have heard the pleas of your people in prayer. Our ships have been in your atmosphere for some time but we are cloaked. We have taken out many of the greys' ships trying to escape Earth's atmosphere. When you are ready, we will make ourselves known."

Esrith raised his hand. "Go ahead, Admiral Esrith," Admiral Tibbets said.

"I can call for volunteers to actively assist your pilots in taking out the greys," he said. He glanced at Thompson.

"I will do the same," Admiral Donner of the Endeavor said.

"As will I," said Admiral Tibbets of the Reliance.

General Thompson stood again and passed around photos of the greys' ships. Admiral Tibbets pulled up holograms of the same ships.

"Thank you, Admiral Tibbets. We are currently holding tribunals for those who were involved in treason and crimes against humanity. These will be televised as soon as we are ready to go public," Thompson added.

The Andromedan Councilor raised his hand. Admiral Tibbets nodded.

"I am Sola. Have you made contingencies for the clones?"

"Yes. We have been arresting them as well. We had over 400,000 indictments that have gone out. When these are all accomplished, then we will be ready to go public," Thompson said.

"How will you notify the public?" Admiral Donner asked.

"We will take over the airways and other devices and shut them down before broadcasting the truth and displaying the tribunals," Admiral Johnson of the U.S. Space Force said.

"We will need to work with your command centers to coordinate our tactics for addressing the problem of the greys' ships," Admiral Halsey of the U.S. Navy said.

"That is acceptable. We will recess for 30 minutes while those divisions remain here to work out the details," Admiral Tibbets said.

Travel Portals

He stood at the bridge of the Reliance, waiting to go through the portal to return to his own ship when he got an urgent call on his comm link.

"Go ahead," he said.

"Admiral Esrith, we just got an emergency signal from CMO Conn," the Ensign said.

"What's her location?"

"She's at the White House."

"See if you can contact the other CMOs. I'm heading to the Concordance now. Call a meeting of all pilots to the map room."

"Yes, sir."

He stood in the portal, along with another officer returning to the Concordance. In a moment, he stood in the portal on his own bridge.

"Any word from Conn or the others?" He left the portal and headed to the Comms board.

"We can't hail the others, sir. There's no signal from them. What should I do about Conn?"

"She may be in danger if we hail her. Keep watching her signal. I'll send her some help." He turned to leave.

"Sir! I've got visual," the Ensign said.

He turned back to the board and viewed what Conn

witnessed. Two large reptilians stood on a table, towering over her. He could hear others whispering nearby. There was no sign of security.

"What do you want from us?" he heard Conn call out.

"We know why you are here. We will stop you." The first reptilian said.

"Damn! Looks like we will have to adjust our plan or switch to another plan altogether. I'll be in the map room. Have you informed the pilots?" he asked.

"Yes Admiral. They should be on their way."

"Let me know if you hear anything else from Conn or the others."

"Yes sir."

When he arrived at the map room, several pilots went inside just before he got to the door.

"Pilots, I need volunteers to help the Federation take out the greys' ships," he said.

All hands shot up.

"Are you all sure?"

"Yes, sir!" the group said in unison.

"You will be under the Federation control, so you must follow their orders." He glanced at his chrono. "You've got five minutes to grab your gear and another five minutes to be ship ready." His comm link beeped. "Dismissed."

Everyone stood up and headed out the door.

"Go ahead," he said into his comm link.

"Sir, two assistants to CMO Shim said they had a faster way to detect Draco Reptilians."

"Patch them through."

"They're here, sir, on the bridge."

"Coming right up."

"What have you got for me?" Esrith asked. He was slightly out of breath after taking the stairs. The people mover had been filled with pilots.

"I'm Datu, and this is Zohn. We have found a spray that will do the job much faster than the blood test. It will penetrate the skin."

"Do you have enough of it to use now? On a lot of people?"

"Yes Admiral. We worked day and night to perfect it."

"Good, I've got to get word to our new partners. Come with me."

He walked out of the bridge area and spotted Eno in the hallway. "Are you sure about this?" he asked his son.

"Yes sir. I'm ready."

He gave Eno's shoulders a squeeze. "I'm proud of you, son."

"I know, sir. And I know how much you'd like to be in my place right now, fighting the greys."

"You're damn right, but I had my time when I was your age. Now I'm called to do other things. Come with me."

"Where are we going?" Eno asked.

"We are going to recruit some help," he said.

Eno, Datu, and Zohn followed behind his long strides. They didn't have to go far, since they headed down the hall.

The door to the Officer's Lounge hissed open. There, at the center table, sat Captain Tremol and his mate Keely, a former Secret Service Agent; Captain Gadara and her mate Torren Conley, a former NASA Astronaut; and Adam and his mate Genesis, a Bounty Hunter for the I.S.P.

"We just got word from the Reliance that their scientists have created a mist that will penetrate the skin of non-humans and expose who they really are. It's much quicker than the blood tests." He stood beside their table.

"Something tells me there's bad news with this," Adam said.

"You're right, Adam. The word from Conn is the damn reptiles have taken over the White House."

3

THE WHITE HOUSE

The third reptilian awoke, while the one at the door was still out. Conn glanced at her chrono, which was next to her comms unit. In a few more minutes, the other one would awaken and then the other after that. She had to come up with a way to escape. But how?

"What did I miss?" Number three asked.

"Nothing here, but they're sending a Blackhawk to the roof." Number one replied. He pressed his clawed hand against his ear. They must be communicating with other reptilians, she thought. *Not good.*

"What for?" Number three asked.

"What do you think?"

"The CIA is on it." Number two replied.

"Our guys?" Number three asked.

"Of course." Number one said.

Number two tapped his ear. "Hey, they got it. It's done."

"Your plan didn't work," Number one said to the small group of crying staffers.

"We got snipers, too," Number two said.

Then she heard the crash. All the souls on that craft were

lost and these creatures didn't even care. Conn scratched her head, making sure her comm link was set to record.

"What now?" She asked.

"You have no right to do this to us," a staffer said.

Number one jumped in the man's face. "Do you know what a food chain is?"

The man nodded. She could see his throat swallow hard. Keep calm. She tried sending the message telepathically.

The reptile tore out the man's throat with his claw and drank the blood spewing out while everyone screamed and moved away. She kept her arm up, hoping to send the video. She didn't know if the last one went through. Suddenly, the other two jumped on the table with Number one and the three of them ripped the clothes off the man and tore out his belly.

While they feasted on him, she moved farther away, trying to make it to the door. She found Denton's stunner and grabbed it.

She motioned for the others to go to the door. Silently, they all moved quickly. She carefully unlocked the door, stepping over the fourth reptilian. The three on the table were so focused on their feeding frenzy that they didn't see them escape. She stayed behind, watching the reptilians and making sure everyone was out the door before closing it behind her. All of them ran down the hall until they came to the main entrance.

Agent Smith pulled out his weapon when he saw them. "What's going on? Where's your security?"

"They're either dead or seriously injured. One of your staff was just eaten by the Secret Service agents who barged into the room," she said. "Three are awake now. One will awaken shortly, and the other will be out for another forty-five minutes."

"It was Bill!" one of the women called out. The staff all started talking at once."

"People, please!" Conn shouted. "He needs to get help down here right away. You have been infiltrated by the reptilians. Don't trust anyone," she said to Agent Smith.

He called for help on his device, then escorted the group outside. "Remain calm. I have to take the report."

"They have snipers on the roof," she added.

Within minutes, several agents came around the side of the building and some from within the building. All were heavily armed.

Agent Smith spoke with their leader. Most of them headed down to the meeting room they had evacuated. Some of them stayed with Agent Smith to watch the entrance, while he took the report.

"Where is your President?" she asked.

"He's in a safe location," Smith replied.

"I hope so. The reptilians mentioned their snipers took out a craft and the CIA was on it," she said.

"The CIA?"

Somewhere in D.C.

CMO Shim stood beside CMO Torres and watched helplessly as their security team was shot and killed in front of them.

"Why did you do that? They did nothing to you!" Shim said.

"I can shoot you, too, if that will make you feel better?"

Shim shook his head. What could he do? He was at the mercy of this person. Certainly the President wouldn't set something like this in place? It didn't make sense.

"Set your bags down and back up," the stranger said.

He did as he was told. He glanced at Torres and watched him comply as well.

The man picked up the bags and walked to the building.

"I think we should run," Shim whispered to Torres.

"I agree, as soon as he is inside."

As soon as the man opened the door, Shim turned and ran in the direction they came from. What did he want with their bags? Why was this happening? He didn't know this place or how they got there, but he wanted as far away as he could get. He glanced to his right and Torres ran beside him. The two of them ran until they came to some traffic.

"What now? I don't know where we are or who to trust," Torres said.

"You think I know? We can't communicate with anyone without our comms. I hope Conn is having better luck than we are," Shim said.

"Do you think the reptilians knew what we were doing here?" Torres asked.

"That has to be it. Why would they want our Med bags? We are the healers, those bags only held the test kit for the reptilian DNA."

"He must have been a reptilian," Torres said.

A yellow vehicle pulled up to them on the sidewalk. The glass went down on the side facing them. "Do you fellas need a ride?"

"We need to get to the President's house," Shim said.

"The White House?"

He glanced at Torres. "It was white, wasn't it?"

"Absolutely, yes." Torres said.

"Get in," the man said.

"Do you promise to take us there?" Shim asked.

"Of course. Do you want a ride or not?"

"Yes. We are lost. We don't know where the President's house is from here," Torres said.

"Well, I know how to get there. Are you getting in or not?"

"We don't know how to enter your craft," Shim said. "The last time we entered the black craft, the door was already opened."

"For cryin' out loud. Pull the damn handle," the man said.

Shim glanced at Torres. "What is a damn handle?"

"Try that." Torres pointed to a silver object.

Shim pulled down on the object and the door popped opened.

"Oh." Shim climbed in and Torres followed him.

"That was much easier than I thought," Shim said.

"Now you have to close the door," the man said.

Torres glanced at the door. "Oh, here's another damn handle," he said. He pulled the lever and the door closed.

"So, you boys new in town?" the man asked.

"Yes, to this town and to your planet," Torres said.

"To this planet? That's a new one. So, where are you two from?"

"I'm from Vestra Minor," Shim said. "It's near Vestra Major which was once our home planet. That is, before the exodus."

"Yes, and I'm from Tarsius. They are both in the Vaedra system. However, the exodus took place over a hundred años ago, to be honest. It wasn't a recent event."

"Is that so? So what are you doing here in D.C.?"

"What is D.C.?" Shim asked.

"Oh. That's the nickname to Washington. D.C. stands for the District of Columbia, where Washington is located."

"We are here with a diplomatic group—"

Torres grabbed Shim's arm. "We are part of the diplomatic group. We are here to exchange ideas and technologies."

Shim nodded. "Yes. The Concordance brought back the Earthen delegation that visited our planetary system and we came here as well." There was no need to tell him specifics, especially if he turned out to be reptilian. He could use that against them.

"You don't say." The driver glanced in his rear view mirror at the two of them. "You know, you two look like ordinary humans to me."

"That's because we *are* human. Didn't the President mention that we were here?" Certainly he said something to the public?

"Come to think of it, I did hear something about it on the news. There was talk about a lot of UFO sightings recently."

"What is a UFO?" Torres asked.

"Now that's funny. If you came here from another planet, you must be flying in a ship of some sort, right?"

"We came in a star destroyer," Shim said.

"You shouldn't have mentioned that part," Torres whispered.

"Why not?" Shim asked.

"Yes, why not?" the man asked. "Are you here to destroy the planet?"

"Of course not! We are here to share technology with the people of Earth," Shim said.

"I don't think they have any technology they can share with us, though," Torres whispered.

"Maybe we do," the man said.

"Do what?" Shim asked.

"Maybe we do have technology we can share with you," the man said. "And it's an unidentified flying object."

"What is?" Torres asked.

"You asked me what is a UFO. I'm telling you what it means."

"Well, we identified ourselves before entering your airspace. And we've spoken to your President," Shim said.

"Well, maybe you identified yourselves, but that doesn't mean all those ships up there are doing that," the man said. "Well, here we are, gentlemen."

"Ah, we are at the President's house, Torres," Shim said.

Shim glanced out the window and saw the group of people outside the entrance. He wondered what was going on.

"There's Conn," Torres said as he opened the door. "We must speak with her at once!"

"That'll be $50," the driver said.

Shim followed Torres out the door and closed it. He glanced inside the opened window. "Thank you for the ride and the conversation." He turned to leave.

"Hey wait!" The driver got out. "You two owe me money!" he shouted. He followed them to the entrance.

"You gentlemen owe me money," the driver shouted at them.

"What is money?" Torres asked. He glanced at Shim and then at the man.

"That's not funny. I'm not leaving until I get paid." He continued to follow them to the door.

Agent Smith approached the three men. "Can I help you?"

"Two of them are with me," Conn said, approaching them.

"I need $50 for the cab fare," the driver said.

"Cab fare? I thought the Secret Service drove you to the lab?" Smith glanced at him and Torres.

"Yes, but he drove off after another man approached the craft and nullified our comm links and weapons. Then, he shot our security guards and took our Med bags. We're lucky to be alive," Shim said.

"Yes, we had to run for our lives until this man rescued us." Torres pointed to the driver.

"Oh, dear!" Conn said.

"Well, I didn't really rescue you. I'm a cab driver. I just gave you a lift, that's all."

"If you hadn't shown up when you did, who knows what would have happened to us. We were lost in your D.C. with no way to communicate with our people," Shim said.

"And you did take us here, to the President's house, like you promised," Torres said.

Conn approached the driver and shook his hand. "Thank you for rescuing my counterparts. We are all healers on each of our ships. The ships couldn't function without their Chief Medical Officers."

"Well, I…it was my pleasure," the driver said.

Smith talked on his device and his leader came to them.

"Here you go," Smith's leader handed the driver some green papers and the driver left.

"This is Agent Gowan." Smith introduced his leader to the three of them.

"I apologize for the strange circumstances. I assure you the President wouldn't have sent you to the lab and left you stranded. I will look into that. Right now, we are clearing out the building. I will be sending the staff home soon. Do you have a way to communicate with your ship?" Gowan said.

"Yes, I do. I will contact them at once," Conn said.

While she contacted the Concordance, Shim tried his device once more. "Mine still does not work," he said.

"Mine is broken as well," Torres said.

Suddenly, there was a loud series of noises coming from inside the building. "Everyone down!" Gowan shouted.

❊ 4 ❊

CONCORDANCE, ABOVE EARTH'S MOON

As the volunteers and pilots lined up to go through the portal, Admiral Esrith received word from Conn through the comm board.

His jaw tensed. "We lost six men," he said solemnly.

"Yes sir, but we still have our healers," the Ensign replied.

"Find out what happened with their weapons. We can't have that happen again," Esrith said.

"Yes, sir."

"And prepare to bring them aboard. We'll need a transporter to collect the bodies and identify each one. Send a security team out—"

"But sir, we don't have any available pilots."

"I'll use the volunteers. Get a security team of four to go with them. I'll assemble the pilots to fly the transporters. And find out what that noise was before Conn stopped transmitting."

"Yes, sir."

He and Eno were the last to go through the portal.

• • •

Reliance, Above Earth's Atmosphere

The Ensign on the Reliance stopped him. "All the pilots are meeting in the eating hall for a briefing, sir. The officers are meeting in the Map Room."

"Thank you, Ensign." He turned toward Eno. "Good luck, son." He gave his shoulders a squeeze.

"Thanks, Dad." Eno ran his hand through his hair and watched his father go in the opposite direction. His dad had spent many hours telling stories of how they fought the greys in his younger days. He enjoyed listening to those stories when he was younger. Now, it was his turn to fight the enemy of all humankind.

He headed for the eating hall. All these ships were designed the same, so he knew the way. He was the last to enter the meeting. The place was packed.

"Our targets are these grey ships," the officer began. He tapped a box on the table and a hologram popped up of the ship. The image was elevated enough that he could see the details.

"We'll be sending you all out to different vectors, with the biggest concentration here." The officer tapped the box again and a map of Earth appeared. He pointed to a specific place near the bottom of the map.

"Isn't that Antarctica?" Adam asked.

Eno glanced at Adam and then studied the map again.

"Yes. The greys and reptilians have been working out of that base for centuries, but there are some Earthen races who have been working with them there for nearly a century."

Eno scratched his head. Centuries? They've had the

reptilians here that long and didn't know about it? How could that have happened?

"What will we be doing?" Adam asked.

"All the wedges and wing ships will be shooting down the grey ships. They are trying to escape and use their portals. They are losing the battle for Earth. The American Military has destroyed most of their deep underground tunnels that they have been using all this time to capture and torture children and young women. Some of the Alliance have been assisting them in doing this. Those of you flying the transporters will assist the other two ships in case of injuries or casualties to innocents."

"Did you want us to take prisoners?" Eno asked.

"No, but if the ship you take down has any live enemies, take them out."

"How did they stay hidden all these centuries without Earthens finding out?" Eno asked.

"That's an excellent question," the officer began. He tapped the box once more and a hologram popped up of the shorter grey alien. The same type he had studied while learning to become an officer/pilot.

"These are the small greys. They will work for the highest bidder. They are excellent geneticists and have created hybrids of Earthens and greys, as well as other creatures. They had worked with the reptilians and a group of Earthens since the 1940s in Germany and then they moved to Antarctica at the end of your second world war." The officer glanced at Adam.

He hit the box again and a hologram of the reptilian popped up. "These are the Draco Reptilians. At one time they had wings and flew around Earth in your earliest times. They bred with female Earthens and created a bloodline that goes for centuries."

"Why would a woman breed with a creature like that?"
Eno asked.

"I assure you, it was probably against her will or knowl-
edge of what the creature was." The officer tapped the box
and the image of the hologram shifted into a man. "These
creatures are shape shifters. They feed off negative vibrations or fear and drink blood of children who have been
tortured to get the adrenachrome they need to look younger.
Otherwise, they will feed off the flesh of any human and
drink their blood. These creatures may be on the ships with
the greys. They can shift up to about seven feet tall. Take
precautions."

Eno heard a lot of mumbling as he glanced around the
room. He didn't study the Dracos as much as the greys.
Maybe he should have. They sound more dangerous. At least
the Alliance was involved. That was a good thing for the
Earthens.

"Any more questions?" the officer asked.

"When do we head out?" Someone from the group asked.

"As soon as you port through to your ships and contact
the Central Command. They will give you your vectors one at
a time. If anything happens, stay with your ships so we can
find you. We don't have enough communicators to hand out,
so you'll be dependent on your ship's comm-link."

Everyone stood and headed to the Bridge to use the
portal. They were sending them out by groups to their respective ships. Eno turned to find his friends walking up behind
him. Hopefully, he would be partnered with someone he
knew.

"Did you know about the Draco Reptilians?" he asked
Adam.

"Hell no. Is that what was on the Concordance that
abducted Torren?" Adam asked.

"I remember seeing them before," Torren said as he joined the conversation.

"The Med Bed that Conn put you through opened up your memories," Captain Gadara said to Torren. She put her arm around him.

"I can't get past what that officer said about them breeding with women," Eno said. The thought made him shiver.

"Oh, that was so wrong," Keely said. "No woman, in her right mind, would breed with one of those creatures, Eno. I assure you, she would have to be drugged or raped."

"I agree," Genesis said.

"Are you all flying the transporters?" Eno asked.

"Yes, we go out as a team. Two per ship," Captain Gadara said. "Don't forget what I taught you, Eno," she said.

"How can I forget, Captain Gadara. You drilled it into my head, remember?"

It looked as if each team would be the mated couples. That was good to know. He was glad for them that they each found their own special someone they would be with for life. Being a pilot on a star destroyer had its drawbacks. Sure, he had bragging rights, but meeting a mate, unless she worked on the ship, was hard to do. He signed up for ten anos and he was only four anos in. He would have to wait six more before he could even consider looking for a mate. By that time, those his age would already be taken. He couldn't dwell on that. It only made him depressed.

He wondered if the Reliance and Endeavor had as many volunteers as the Concordance. Of course, none of them had Torren Conley, Captain Tremol and Keely, or Adam and Genesis. They may have their version of Captain Gadara, but he bet none of them were as good looking as she was. Torren was one lucky man.

Finally, it was their turn to port out to the Concordance. They all went as a group. When they landed on the bridge of the Concordance, Eno turned to the group. "After this is over, I'm buying the drinks."

"You got it," Adam said.

Torren did a high five with him. "Not if I buy them first!"

"We'll see about that," Eno said.

He loved this banter among friends. He never realized he had friends before he met Torren Conley. Now, he'd accumulated quite a few.

He led the small group to the flight deck. When he turned around, he realized all the pilots from the Concordance were behind them.

"Good luck everyone," he said. He shook each friend's hand, then stood by his ship and glanced around to the other pilots. He gave them a thumbs up and they returned the gesture. He climbed into his wedge-shaped escort and started pre-flight. Each pilot had to go through pre-flight and seek permission to leave the flight deck. Once that was done, they would head out to the Reliance and receive their vectors.

Just before seeking permission to leave the ship, he glanced up at the Command Center and saw his father, the Admiral, inside. He gave another thumbs up and his father returned the gesture.

"Shadow One to Control," he said.

"Go ahead, Shadow One."

"Request permission to exit the ship."

"Permission granted."

His adrenaline pumped through his veins as he anticipated the combat between the greys and himself. He was ready to kick some alien ass. But first, he headed to the Reliance, which was above Earth's atmosphere. He had to pick up his vector heading. With all the ships coming from the Concordance and those from the Endeavor, the skies around the Reliance were going to be full.

He waited his turn and noticed the ships were sent off in twos. First the wings were sent, then the wedges. There were transporters from each ship, but the Concordance had more of them. That meant they did have pilots to fly them.

His vector heading sent him to a place in New Mexico and he was paired with a wing ship from the Reliance, Ardant One. "Come in Ardant One, this is Shadow One," he said.

"Ardant One, go ahead."

"I'll take the top half of the vector if you'll take the bottom," he said.

"Good deal Shadow One. Will do. Ardant One out."

He flew low over the skies with his ship cloaked. Most of this area seemed to be a desert. Did humans actually live here?

He crisscrossed the skies, making a grid pattern so as not to miss anything. Once he covered his area, he reversed his pattern and went back up.

Finally, something blipped on his Nav-U-Comm screen. He tracked it and picked up movement ahead. The ship he followed was also cloaked, but he had gotten a reading on his sensor, making it appear as a blip. Without visuals, he wasn't sure if it was a grey ship or something else. There was no mention of other ships in the area, except the greys. He stayed with the blip on his sensor and closed the gap between them.

"Central Command, this is Shadow One, do you read?"

"Go ahead, Shadow One."

"I've got a reading on my Nav-U-Comm but no visuals. Been following it a few minutes."

"Is it a sporadic reading or smooth and steady, Shadow One?"

"It's sporadic and hard to keep up with."

"Then it's a grey ship. The Earthens don't have anything capable of that type of flying."

"Got it. Shadow One out."

He moved closer to the object and locked in on the target. He pressed the button on his firing cannon and hit the object. It lit up the screen, but it was still there. Now it appeared to wobble in the Nav-U-Comm. He couldn't see anything visually. After locking on again, he fired once more. This time, a light flashed in the sky and he pulled up. It just missed him.

Another light flashed and he pulled up again, but he took a hit, shaking his ship.

"Whoa!" Could they see him? Did they have a lock on his ship? He locked on to the target once more and fired twice in succession. This time the blip went down and off the screen.

"Central Command this is Shadow One, come in."

No response.

"Central Command this is Shadow One, can you read?"

MERCY, NEW MEXICO

Willow Tree Moon made her rounds in the small town of Mercy, just outside the Mescalero Apache Indian Reservation in New Mexico. She had been with the police department for over a year and the town was usually quiet, but not today.

"421, come in," the dispatcher said.

Willow Tree keyed the mike. "421, go ahead."

"We have a missing child report."

Her heart pounded. This cannot be happening. Not in this little town. She pulled out her pad and took down the address.

"I'm in route." She turned her vehicle around and headed for the subdivision. The town was pretty rural, so everything was spread out. A missing child was rare. At least, she had not heard of one since she had been with the department. She began a slow breath in and exhaled slowly out to calm down. She had to be calm to help the parents.

When she pulled up to the subdivision, two women, standing in the road, flagged her down.

"Are you the persons who reported a missing child?" she asked the two women.

"I am." The taller woman stepped forward. She seemed upset and panicky. The other woman sobbed into a wet tissue and appeared to be shaking.

Willow Tree exited her vehicle and approached the two women, her pad and pen in hand. "What can you tell me about the incident," she said.

"I was out front with my daughter and her child." She pointed to the woman next to her.

"Let me get your name first," Willow Tree said. She jotted down both names and their addresses. "Go ahead."

"Like I said, I was outside with the two girls when my daughter said she was thirsty. So I went inside to get them some water. When I came out, they were both gone."

"How long were you inside?" Willow Tree asked her.

"About five minutes."

"Did you see or hear any vehicles in your neighborhood?" Willow Tree asked.

"No. And I called Amy and asked if the girls went over to her house."

"How old are the girls?"

"Maria is five and Tasha is four."

"Did you see or hear anything?" she asked the second mother.

"No," she sobbed. "I was doing laundry."

"I'll need a description of what they were wearing. Do you have any recent photos of them?"

The taller woman, Mrs. Gonzalez, gave a description of the clothing, while Mrs. Taylor went to grab a photo. She jotted down the description and Mrs. Taylor handed her the picture.

"The blonde is Tasha, and the brunette is María."

Willow Tree took down the two women's phone numbers

and then contacted her dispatcher with a description for an APB.

"I've got an APB out for the girls. In the meantime, I'll take a walk around your neighborhood to see if I can find them or if anyone has seen them." She handed a business card to each woman. "Be sure and call me if the girls come home."

"Yes, officer. Please find them. They've never wandered off before," Mrs. Gonzalez said.

Willow Tree locked up her vehicle and took her portable with her, clipping it to her belt. She walked around each house, front and back and up and down the street. She knocked on doors. Most people were at work at this hour, so she had no luck with anyone being home, until she knocked on the last door.

The woman who answered the door had seen something odd.

"Yes, I saw a UFO land just down the street." She pointed to the Gonzalez house. "I called it in to the police. I even drew a picture of it." She handed the picture to Willow Tree.

How odd that the dispatcher hadn't called her on the radio since it was in the same neighborhood.

"May I keep this?" Willow Tree asked.

"Sure."

"How long was the UFO there?"

"About a minute or two. It hovered more than landed."

"We have a couple of missing little girls in your neighborhood."

"Oh my."

Willow Tree handed her a business card. "If you remember anything else, or if you see the ship again, call me direct on my cell phone."

"I sure will."

When Willow Tree reached her vehicle, she waited until she was inside to contact the dispatcher.

"Go ahead," the dispatcher responded.

"Did you get any calls about a UFO sighting in the Sunset Subdivision?"

"Yes. We had two of them within minutes of each other."

"Did you happen to get the addresses of the callers?"

"No, you know those kooks just call in stuff like that for fun."

"You *do* realize that may have something to do with the missing children in the same neighborhood?"

No response. Willow Tree pounded the steering wheel. How could the dispatcher dismiss these calls? She would definitely mention that in her report. But how could she track a UFO? What good would that do? At least she had a drawing. "God, I need your help on this one," she prayed. The two mothers had been frantic. She would be too, if that was her daughter. How can she follow up if aliens were involved? She headed back to the station.

She worked for a good forty-five minutes getting the details right in the report. She mentioned the dispatcher's negligence. So what if Carmela *was* the niece of the Police Chief.

She handed her report to the Chief. "That's my report on the missing children. I just don't know how to follow up on this."

He glanced at the report. "This looks like a dead end, Willow Tree. We'll have to file it in the open cases file and hope for the best."

"Could you let me know if we have any more UFO sightings in that area?" Willow Tree asked.

"I'll let Carmela know, but I don't see how that will help anything."

"Yes sir." She left the office. She had a few spiritual gifts up her sleeve that the Chief didn't know about, but could those gifts help her with this case?

Eno tracked the grey's ship on his Nav-U-Comm as it went down in the desert area of New Mexico. He must have damaged their cloaking device because now he could see their ship. He tried his comms once more.

"Shadow One to Central Command, come in."

No response.

"Damn!" He had no comms. How was he going to let anyone know where to find him? He'd have to figure that out later. Right now, he needed to make sure there were no grey survivors.

Through his viewport, he caught a glimpse of people running from the desert to a road, but something held the greys' ship off the ground. He de-cloaked his own ship and landed nearby in the dirt. He grabbed his cannon and exited his ship through the lowering ramp.

Willow Tree drove down the highway to the outskirts of town on her regular patrol. Off in the distance, she saw a small family hiking through an open area with scrub brush and some cactus. It appeared they were about to have a picnic. She caught a glimpse of something moving overhead.

"Oh no, a UFO." She pulled up behind the vehicle parked alongside the road. The UFO resembled the drawing the woman had given her earlier.

"421 to dispatch," she called on the radio.

"Go ahead."

"I'm checking out a UFO off Hwy 54."

"What was that?"

Willow Tree didn't respond. She grabbed her portable, clipped it on her belt and pulled her weapon out of its holster. She ran toward the family in the field. They were oblivious to what was going on overhead. She saw flashes of light coming from something she couldn't see and from the UFO.

"Hey!" she shouted to the family.

The mother turned toward her. She waved her arm, motioning for them to come to her, then pointed to the sky.

The mother glanced up, froze and screamed. The father and kids looked up and started screaming. Willow Tree motioned again for them to come toward her. All at the same time, the family ran her way.

"Get in your car and get out of here," she shouted.

She noticed a couple more flashes and the UFO came down fast. She holstered her gun and used her telekinetic powers to hold the ship in place so it couldn't land. Suddenly, another ship appeared nearby. It was shaped like a triangle. It landed several feet away from the UFO she held in place. When she saw a human male exit the triangle, she dropped the first UFO down hard, shaking the ground slightly.

She had to see if the girls were inside. *Dear God, let them be all right.* The tall, blond man walked toward the UFO and shot at it with a strange weapon he held on his shoulder. A large hole opened up with the blast.

She walked toward him. "I'm looking for two small girls," she said.

He blasted the UFO again and a ramp opened up. She pulled her weapon out and followed him up the ramp. He fired again and two grey creatures fell off the ramp.

He bent over and picked up their weapons. "Here, hold these," he said.

She quickly holstered her weapon and took the new weapons in her hands and followed him into the ship. There, in the center, was some kind of computerized circular unit with seats surrounding it. Off to the side was a cage with the two little girls.

"Oh my God." She ran to them, set the weapons down, and checked their pulses. They were alive, but not moving. Their eyes were closed.

The man moved toward the girls and picked up one of the weapons she had set down. He shot at the cage door and it disappeared.

She scooped up María and a weapon and took her outside. She lay her on the ground so she could heal her. The man set Tasha down beside María.

"I'll be right back. I'm going to see if they have any other prisoners," he said. She had to crane her neck to look up to him.

Willow Tree began her praying and laying on of hands. She started with María and then moved on to Tasha.

"I want my mommy," Tasha cried out when she awoke.

"I will get you to your mommy. Are you both all right?"

Both girls nodded.

Willow Tree called the dispatcher on the radio. "421 to dispatch."

"Go ahead. Are you still chasing UFOs?" Carmela laughed.

"Contact the parents of María Gonzalez and Tasha Taylor and have them meet me at the hospital. Their phone numbers are in my report."

"10-4."

She returned her radio to her belt and helped the girls stand up. "Can you walk to my cruiser?" she asked.

Both girls nodded.

The blond man walked down the ramp.

"Any more people in there?" she asked.

He shook his head. "Just a few body parts."

"What?"

He moved beside her and whispered in her ear. "They were half eaten. Greys don't usually eat human flesh. I checked their mouths. They were hybrids."

"I'm sorry you had to see that," she said. "I want to thank you for helping me find the girls."

"You're welcome." He reached out and touched her arm. "How did you stop that ship from landing?"

"Telekinesis." She pulled out her card and handed it to him. "If you need to contact me, I'm Willow Tree Moon."

She held both girls' hands and walked back to her vehicle. The family was long gone. Thank goodness she didn't have any one else go missing. She got the girls into the car and buckled them in. Once she was inside, she called the dispatcher. "421 to dispatch."

"Oh, thank goodness. Go ahead."

"I'm leaving the scene and heading to the hospital."

"About that," the dispatcher started. "I couldn't find your report."

"Did you contact the parents?"

"No, because I couldn't find your report."

She remembered the girls in the back seat and kept her cool. This was obviously an incompetent dispatcher. She took a deep breath and let it out twice before responding.

"Ask the Chief. I gave him the report." She released the mike. Why was that so hard to figure out?

"Are you girls comfortable?"

"I want my mommy," Tasha cried.

"We will see your mommy at the hospital." She glanced around her vehicle. She always made copies of her reports. There it was, in her clipboard. She pulled out the report and dialed María's mother first, then Tasha's mother. "I need you to meet me at the hospital. Everything is fine and I found your daughter alive."

While she headed to the hospital, she asked the girls some questions. "Did those creatures hurt you?" She glanced in the rearview mirror for their reactions.

"They put something in our arms," María said.

"It hurt, too." Tasha said.

"Did they touch you anywhere else?"

"No. They just grabbed me like this," María demonstrated on Tasha, twisting her grip.

"Ouch!" Tasha said.

"Then they stuck that thing against our arms, and put us in the cage. I got real sleepy."

I'm sorry that happened to you," Willow Tree said. "Are you girls thirsty or hungry?"

"I'm thirsty," Tasha said.

"Me, too," María said.

Willow Tree pulled up to the parking lot at the hospital. "I'll get you some water inside." She unbuckled the girls and helped them out of the vehicle. As they walked toward the entrance, a shadow ran across her arms. She glanced up and saw the triangular-shaped craft she had seen before. The girls clung to her and started screaming.

"It's okay," she said. She squatted down and hugged both of them. "He's a good guy. He helped me rescue you from the bad creatures."

She watched with the girls as the craft set down in a field

beside the parking lot. The ramp went down and he stepped out of his ship.

"Willow Tree Moon," he called out.

"Right here!" She raised her hands somewhat, still clinging to the two frightened little girls. He trotted toward them.

"I meant to ask you if the girls received implants," he said.

"From what they told me, yes. We were about to go inside to see if their parents are here. I'd like the doctors to check them as well."

"On our ship, the Concordance, we have Med Beds that can diagnose and remove implants. If they aren't removed, the girls can be tracked and the aliens will come back for them."

"I thought we took care of that problem."

"I assure you, there are more greys on this planet."

"Oh, my." Willow Tree noticed the girls were calm now and craning their heads to see this very tall, good looking man. She was six foot and she still had to look up into his pale blue eyes.

"Why don't you come inside with us while I look for their parents. We'd have to get their permission to do that."

"Sure." He turned and pointed something at the ship and it disappeared.

The entrance door to the hospital opened and they all walked inside.

"I didn't get your name," she said to the tall man.

"Eno ni Esrith."

"Can you wait here with the girls and I'll get them some water."

"My pleasure," he said. The girls grabbed Eno's hands as soon as she broke free.

Willow Tree spoke to someone at the desk and got the information she needed. She found the drink machine and brought back four bottles of water. As she handed out the waters, both sets of parents came through the door.

"Mommy!" Both girls yelled at the same time. They ran to their respective parents.

She took a big swallow of her water and watched the tearful reunion.

"Can we take them home now?" Mr. Gonzalez asked.

"I brought them here with the intention of having the doctors check them out, but this gentleman says he has access to some Med Beds."

Everyone looked up to Eno. "I'm stationed on the Concordance and we do have Med Beds there that can analyze and diagnose anything that could be wrong with a human and then fix the problem. The reason I mentioned the Med Beds is because the girls were abducted by the greys and they use implants to track the people they've abducted and then pick them up again and again."

"What is the Concordance?" Mr. Taylor asked.

"It's one of the Star Force's fourteen ships that patrol the Vaedran galaxy."

Both sets of parents took a step back, pulling the girls with them.

"Are you saying you aren't from Earth?" Mrs. Taylor asked.

❧ 6 ❧

MERCY HOSPITAL, MERCY, NEW MEXICO

"I am Lieutenant Eno ni Esrith, an officer and pilot for the Vaedran Star Force. We are here, along with the Earth Alliance and the Galactic Federation of Worlds, to help you fight the greys and reptilians who have taken over your planet."

"You're telling us that aliens have taken over our planet?" Mr. Taylor asked.

"Yes. They have been here for centuries, but your military has been working hard to stop them. These are the Dark Forces trying to escape your Earth."

"There has been more UFO activity lately. Is that what's happening?" Willow Tree asked.

"Yes." He glanced at her.

"Well, how do we get the girls to your ship?" Mr. Gonzalez asked.

"I can take only up to four people in my ship. My comm-link is down and I can't contact anyone. I'm not sure if my ship is space-capable after sustaining some damage."

"How can we help you?" Willow Tree asked. She touched his arm to reassure him and his biceps muscle twitched.

"Why are you trying to help an alien?" Mr. Taylor asked.

"Because he helped me find your daughter, Mr. Taylor."

"Jimmy, stop. Tasha is alive and safe. I will help you if I can," Mrs. Taylor said.

"We can help, too," Mrs. Gonzalez said.

"I need to repair my comm-link. I can call for a transporter that will bring everyone to the Concordance at the same time, and return everyone back to Earth when the implants have been removed."

"Let's go, then," Willow Tree said. She ushered the small group outside and through the parking lot to where Eno had landed his ship.

He pressed a device in his hand and the cloaking disappeared so they could see his ship.

"Wow! That is so awesome," Mr. Taylor said.

"I've never seen anything like it," Mr. Gonzalez said.

"Well, these are the ships that belong to the good guys. The grey's ships are round," Eno said.

Once he opened the ramp with the same device, the three men went inside.

She glanced around and watched the two mothers usher the girls into their respective vehicles.

Her curiosity made her continue up the ramp. She wanted to see what the inside of Eno's ship looked like. Was it different from the grey's ship? It actually looked more like a jet inside, with seating for four and a little more room. Nothing like what she saw in the grey's interior.

"I've been trying to put the wires together, but I don't have enough to fix what was destroyed." Eno said.

"Let me have a look at it," Mr. Gonzalez said. He studied the exposed wires and the things they were attached to. "I work on cars. Maybe I can get you some wire," Gonzalez said.

"Thank you," Eno said.

"How are you going to plug the hole underneath the wires?" Mr. Taylor asked.

"Hole?" Eno studied the area Mr. Taylor pointed to. "I missed that. Thanks for finding it. I may have a patch that will work." Eno moved to the back of the ship, behind the last two seats, and opened a container, pulling something out, along with some tools. He began working on the patch.

"I'm going to head to the garage and see what I can find along the lines of wiring," Mr. Gonzalez said. "How long will you be here?"

"As long as it takes," Eno said. He stood holding a couple of pieces of strange looking metal and something like a thick marker.

"Here's my card," Willow Tree handed it to Mr. Gonzalez. "Let me know if you can help him and I'll get the information to Eno."

"I'll be back too. I want to get Tasha and my wife home for now and I'll be back to help you." Mr. Taylor followed Mr. Gonzalez out of the ship. She watched them walk to their vehicles and get inside.

"What can I help you with?" Willow Tree asked. His friendly demeanor encouraged her to stick around.

"If you can go outside and see if you can find any other holes, I can fix them before the men come back."

"You got it." She went down the ramp and walked around the ship. She ran her hand over the surface to see if she could feel something she might over look. The only spot she found was the same hole Eno patched on the inside.

"Eno?"

"I can hear you."

"Yes. It looks like the hole is much bigger on the outside."

"Thank you. I will bring plenty of material."

She waited outside for a few minutes before Eno came with the packet of materials.

"How can you patch something like a space ship to make it safe to fly?"

"I'll show you." He aimed a small device around the outside of the hole. It was the object that looked like a thick marker. He quickly placed a piece of metal-like substance over the hole. Then he aimed the device at the outside of the metal and it flowed like liquid, smoothing out and becoming one with the rest of the ship. In seconds, it appeared as if nothing had ever been damaged.

"Oh my gosh! I wish I could do that to my car where someone backed into it."

"Is your car made of this same material?"

"I don't know, what is this?" She smoothed her hand over the spot he worked on and it was cool to the touch.

"It is an alloy made up of metals and minerals found in space. We keep extra packets on each ship in case we sustain damage from asteroids or beam weapons."

"Well, my car is not made from space material, so I guess it won't work."

Eno glanced at his watch. "The Admiral must be frantic since I haven't been able to contact the Concordance or Central Command."

"I wish I could help you there, but this radio doesn't work much further than the county. The only thing I can think of is to contact the military and see if they can contact your people."

"Not all your military is good. If you notify the black hats, they may try to dispose of me and this ship."

"What do you mean by black hats?"

"Some of your military is working with the reptilians and

greys. They could also *be* reptilians that shifted into human form. That's why these creatures have been able to take over your planet."

"If they are doing that, how would we even know?" she said.

"That's why your planet needs help. The Galactic Federation has dealt with the Dark Forces before. There are so many here that you couldn't possibly take them all out yourselves, especially if you've never dealt with them before."

"This is so overwhelming. I mean, I fought in Iraq and I knew who the enemy was, but this? If they look human and act human, how can I tell if they aren't?" she asked.

"Our Chief Medical Officers from each ship went to your White House to help the President determine who was human and who was reptilian, but some of his agents attacked them after shifting into reptilians."

"Oh, no! I can't believe it's gotten that bad. Most people have no idea this has been going on. I wish there was something I could do."

"You are doing something, right now. You're helping me fix my ship. You've convinced two people to help me who might not have, on their own. Plus, you rescued two little girls from the greys," Eno said.

"I couldn't have done it without your help and you know it."

Eno went back up the ramp and she followed him. "Tell me, Eno, how did this Federation know we needed help? Are they living here on the planet as humans or something?"

"No. Well, there probably are aliens living here that *are* humans, they just come from other planets. The Federation is full of beings who are more spiritual or telepathic in nature and they heard your people cry out in prayer. That's why they stepped in to help."

"How do you know this?"

"They talked about this on Vaedra when your dignitaries and Joint Chiefs of Staff visited our system. The Pleiadians were there and that's when they convinced us to step in and help the Earth Alliance. Plus, the Admiral of the Concordance happens to be my father."

"Oh, so you're privy to some good intel, then."

"You could say that, yes."

"So, how did you get this mission?"

"I volunteered, like all the pilots on the Concordance, the Reliance and the Endeavor. We know what the greys are capable of and we all wanted to kick some alien ass."

"I'll bet. If I had known about them earlier, I would have done the same thing. The only problem is, our government has lied to us about their existence for years. Now, it seems they lied about a lot of other things as well."

"From what I've been hearing, your government, or I should say, the white hats, are planning full disclosure of all the truth."

"That will be a day to celebrate."

"When that happens, if I'm still here, I'll buy you a drink," he said.

"I'd like that." She watched him put up his tools and material, then glanced at her watch. "I'm on overtime and I need to work on my report. I'll be in my vehicle if you need me."

He turned toward her. "Are you leaving then?"

"No. I'll stay here to make sure Mr. Gonzalez and Mr. Taylor come back."

"Thank you. You've been very kind."

"Hey, that's the least I could do since you helped me recover two little girls." She smiled and headed down the ramp.

She felt a bounce in her step at the thought of his warm smile and his pale blue eyes. She just couldn't get over how tall he was. Even she had to look up into his eyes. She wasn't used to that. Most men, if they were tall, were about her height, but not this guy. He was a good head taller than she was. It was actually refreshing.

Concordance

"Central Command to Shadow One. Can you read me?"

"Has he responded?" Admiral Esrith asked.

"No sir. He's the only one. The rest have taken down several grey ships each and reported in."

"Send one of the transporters to his location. There must be something there to locate him." Admiral Esrith paced back and forth.

"Yes, sir. Transporter Three, come in."

"Transporter Three, go ahead," Captain Tremol said.

"We've lost communications with Shadow One. His signal went out at the same time as his comms."

"What was his last location?"

"I'll send his last coordinates to your Nav-U-Comm. Contact me as soon as you have a visual. Central Command out."

Transporter Three

Captain Tremol turned to his mate, Keely. "We need to head west."

"Where are we going?" She glanced at the coordinates on the Nav-U-Comm.

He tapped some keys on the pad and a map popped up.

"New Mexico?" Keely asked.

"Yes. We've been there before, haven't we?"

"Yes, we have. Remember our first adventure searching for the landing party?"

"How can I forget? That's when I fell in love with you," Tremol said.

"Are you sure it wasn't when you showed me how human you really were?"

He glanced at her and smiled. "That's when I made love to you. I fell for you when we hid together in the ship."

"Oh, you remember the very moment you fell for me?"

"Yes. Don't you remember when you fell for me?"

"Of course I do." Keely said.

"Well?"

"Well, what?"

"When was it?"

"It's when you made love to me. I thought you knew that."

"Well, now I do."

It was several minutes before he was over the target area.

"I'm not getting any readings," Keely said.

"Me, either. We should at least pick up his signal."

Tremol flew from the northern part of the state all the way to the southern part, making a zigzag pattern, trying to pick up something.

"Not even a blip," Keely said.

"Let's try it again. We'll just reverse direction," Tremol said.

"Good idea," Keely said.

After another thirty minutes, there was still no sign of Eno. Keely checked the monitor and readings on the Nav-U-Com.

"I have a bad feeling about this."

MERCY HOSPITAL PARKING LOT, NEW MEXICO

Willow Tree jumped when her cell phone rang. She was sitting in her patrol vehicle, about halfway through the report.

"Hello?"

"Officer Moon?"

"Yes."

"This is Jorge Gonzalez. I found some wire and I have my tools. I should be there in a few minutes. Is the alien still there?"

"His name is Eno and yes. I'm here, too."

"Good. See you soon."

She put her clipboard away. She would have to finish this report sometime later today. With everything that was going on, she really doubted that, but she had to have some semblance of a plan. She exited her vehicle and headed to Eno's ship.

"Hello?" she called up to him from the bottom of the ramp. Eno ducked his head through the entrance and smiled. He had a nice smile, too.

"Good news! Mr. Gonzalez is heading this way with some wire and tools."

"Thank you. I really appreciate this. I feel helpless without my comms unit."

"I know the feeling. I would be lost without my radio," she said. Although Eno didn't look helpless at all.

When Mr. Gonzalez pulled up, Mr. Taylor was with him.

She stood by the ramp while the three men worked on the wiring. It was way too crowded with all of them inside, working at the same time, especially at the controls.

"421, come in," dispatch said. She realized it was a male voice. She glanced at her watch. It was 4:00 p.m. She should have been off at 3:30 p.m. It was David Enlow, the evening dispatcher.

"421, go ahead."

"I was checking to make sure you were all right. I see that you didn't sign off on your shift."

"Thank you for checking on me. I'm finishing up my report of today's incidents and I'll drop them off on my way home."

This was a good time to finish up the report since the three men were busy working on the ship. She slipped back into her vehicle and pulled up her clipboard. She picked up where she left off and continued until she finished. When she glanced up, the three men walked down the ramp. They didn't look happy.

She stepped out of the vehicle.

"Were you able to fix it?" she asked.

"I think something is missing," Mr. Gonzalez replied.

"He's right. And I'm also missing the transponder that gives off my signal," Eno said.

"Without the modulator, he won't be able to communicate with his people," Mr. Taylor said.

"Well, thank you both for trying. We'll think of something." She scratched her head. How could she make this up to him? What would she do if she couldn't communicate with anyone herself?

She watched the men drive off. "I've got to drop off this report after making copies of it, then I'll head home. Why don't you follow me in your ship."

"Sure. I'll use the cloaking so I won't be spotted by the greys."

"Good idea."

She pulled out onto the highway and headed to the police station downtown. She watched Eno's ship take off and disappear.

What other ways could she communicate besides her radio and her phone? Then it hit her. She was telepathic. Was anyone Eno knew telepathic as well? She would find out once they stopped at her house.

Would her parents accept him as readily as she did? With her family's background, she thought they certainly *would* accept him. She would soon find out.

She pulled into the parking lot at the station. The Chief was off, so she made copies of her report and then placed the original in his box. She put her copy into her clipboard and headed back to the parking lot.

She would fill the Chief in tomorrow. Right now, she was hungry and had an alien to deal with. She went back out to her vehicle and drove home. Since it was a small town and there were times when they got called in when they were off duty, they were each allowed to drive a cruiser home.

Hopefully, Eno wouldn't get lost. She pulled into the driveway about ten minutes later.

When she got inside, her mother greeted her from the kitchen. "Hello honey! You're late today."

"Hi, Mom. I brought home a guest."

Yellow Elk looked past her. "Where is your guest?"

She walked past her mother and out the back door to the porch. "He should be landing about now," she called out. She took off her gun belt and set it on one of the lounge chairs on the porch. Then she stood there, watching the ground around their back yard. The sand moved ever so slightly, just beyond the house.

"There he is." She pointed to where she had seen the movement.

Yellow Elk was behind her. "I don't see anything. What are you talking about?"

A ramp appeared, then Eno stepped down the ramp.

"That's weird." Yellow Elk said. She cocked her head at what she witnessed.

"This is Eno ni Esrith, my guest." She felt herself smile. Something she hadn't done in a while. Her mother caught her smile and gave her a puzzled look.

Eno looked toward the porch and noticed them staring. He waved and headed over.

Bear Hunter, her father, walked out onto the porch behind them. "What's going on?"

"We are watching for Willow Tree's guest," Yellow Elk said.

"Eno, this is my father, Bear Hunter Moon and my mother, Yellow Elk Moon. Mom and Dad, this is Eno ni Esrith."

"Nice to meet you both." He reached his hand out to Bear Hunter and shook hands. Then he did the same for Yellow Elk. "I'm sorry to impose but my ship's communications are down and my transponder is missing. My people won't be able to locate me without it."

"You say you have a ship?" Bear Hunter asked.

"Yes, sir. Oh, I forgot." Eno turned and pressed a device he held in his hand, and his ship re-emerged.

"Ah. It is a smart-looking ship," Bear Hunter said.

"It looks more like our military jets," Yellow Elk said.

"You have jets that look like this?" Eno asked.

"Well, sort of," Yellow Elk said. "I must get back to my kitchen." She turned and left the porch.

"You know, we should go back to that field and see if we can find those items." Willow Tree couldn't resist touching his thick biceps again, pretending to lead him into the house.

"That's such a big place to search," he said, looking into her eyes.

"Well, that grey ship will be easy to spot so we could start there. Besides, we don't have any other options unless you like being stranded." They stepped over the threshold and into the house.

"Willow Tree?" Bear Hunter called out.

"Yes, sir?" She turned to see him holding her service belt.

"Oh my gosh! I completely forgot." She let go of Eno's arm and retrieved her belt with her gun and radio still attached.

"Thanks, Dad." She turned and blushed, walking past Eno and Yellow Elk and into her bedroom. She set the belt down on her bed. How could she be so careless? She usually never took off her belt except in her bedroom. She quickly changed clothes and regained her composure, then went back into the dining room.

"Come along, I have dinner ready," Yellow Elk said. She ushered them to the table. "You can sit here," Willow Tree said to Eno. She sat across from him and her parents sat across from each other. Once they were situated at the table, Bear Hunter started with the questions.

"I take it you are from another galaxy?"

"Yes sir, the Vaedra system. It's actually closer than the Andromeda system."

"Welcome to our home. Our ancestors came from another galaxy, from the planet Matta."

Yellow Elk took Willow Tree's hand and Eno's hand. Willow Tree took Bear Hunter's hand and Bear Hunter took Eno's other hand.

"We give thanks to the Great Spirit for this food. Bless this food and our bodies for your service. Amen."

Yellow Elk passed the bread, while Bear Hunter passed the venison. Willow Tree passed the vegetables.

"This is interesting food," Eno said. He took a bite of his meat. "What kind of meat is this?"

"Venison," Bear Hunter said.

"It reminds me of an animal I've eaten on Chroma, my home planet."

"Why are you here?" Bear Hunter asked. He took a bite of his steamed vegetables.

"I came with a delegation of Counselors from the Vaedra system and several Earth delegates we were returning when Adam, one of your Earthens, had a premonition that Earth was under attack. We then contacted our allies, the Pleiadians, and they urged us to help the Earth Alliance in fighting the Dark Fleet that was trying to destroy your Earth. I came on the Concordance and we brought two more ships with us to help in the battle for Earth." Eno looked mostly at Bear Hunter when he spoke, but glanced at Willow Tree a couple times. He tried a bite of the vegetables.

"So how did you get into your predicament with your ship's communications?" Yellow Elk asked. Willow Tree sat up and took a bite of her venison. This was where they met.

"I was sent to take down the greys' ships. I'm working

with Central Command of the Galactic Federation of Worlds and your military."

"I thought you said some of the military can't be trusted," Willow Tree said.

"There are good people, the white hats, and bad people, the black hats, in your military. If you don't know who you're talking to, then you could be in trouble. I've spoken with your Joint Chiefs of Staff who are running missions here on Earth. They've mostly completed wrapping up the sex trafficking part of it and now they want us to take out the greys' ships as they try to leave Earth. I was assigned to this vector."

"But how did you lose your communications?" Bear Hunter asked.

"Well, when I shot down the greys' ship, they hit me at the same time. My ship was cloaked, so I don't know how they found me, but they put a hole in my ship, which is how I lost my transponder and the modulator." He stopped and glanced at Willow Tree. "That's when I met your daughter. She held the greys' ship in place and I was able to finish them off."

"What?" Bear Hunter glanced at her.

"I saw a family walking out into the field. It looked as if they were about to have a picnic when I saw the UFO. I had to warn them because I had a missing child report this morning and a UFO was spotted in the vicinity."

"You could have been hurt," Yellow Elk said, looking at her.

"Yes, and that family could have ended up like the two little girls. I held the ship in place because I thought they were trying to escape and I wanted to see if the children were in the ship."

"If she hadn't done that, they could have gotten away."

Eno said. "I was able to finish off the two greys and she found the two children."

"You found children on the ship?" Bear Hunter asked.

"Yes. We got them off the ship and I healed them but Eno thinks they may have implants."

"We need to get them to the Concordance so they can be placed in the Med Beds. The Medical staff can locate the implants and remove them." Eno said.

"That's why I'm going to help Eno find his transponder and modulator, so he can communicate with his people," she said.

When they finished dinner, Yellow Elk spoke. "You will stay here tonight. In the morning, Willow Tree will help you find your equipment."

Transporter Three

By the time Tremol and Keely searched New Mexico twice, it was dark.

"I think we should try searching in the morning," Keely said.

"You're right. I can't seem to pick up a signal out here."

"I just hope Eno is all right," Keely said.

❧ 8 ❧

THE WHITE HOUSE

"CMO Conn to the Concordance, come in."

"Go ahead, Conn."

"There's a battle going on here at the President's home with the Earthen military and the reptilians. We need evacuation."

"We're sending someone there now, Conn. Hold on."

"Thank you!"

She glanced at her two counterparts. "How are we going to get to the outside from here?"

They were inside a bunker with all the Vaedran dignitaries, Earthen delegates, the President and his staff, and a few of his Secret Service agents, along with military people guarding all entrances.

"Hopefully, they will send Vaedran security to retrieve us," Shim said.

Reliance, Admiral Tibbets' Map Room

"We'll need a transporter at the White House to pick up

our CMOs and dignitaries," Tibbets said to the Central Command.

"I got word from the Concordance that a battle is going on there with the military and the reptilians," Admiral Esrith said.

"We can send a cloaked security team there to take out the reptilians, if that will help?" Tibbets said.

"I'm sure it will," Esrith said. "And I need a transporter to pick up the bodies of our fallen teammates."

"Tibbets to Central Command. Send two cloaked security teams down to the White House to help take out the reptilians and pick up the bodies of our fallen heroes. They will answer to the Earthen military leader."

"You got it! Central Command out."

Concordance

"Captain Tremol, any news on Shadow One?" Central Command asked.

"No sir. We're done for the day. We will search again in the morning."

Tremol pulled into the bay and set the transporter down. "I pray that Eno is safe," Keely said, getting out of the ship.

Tremol and Keely headed to the Lounge to see if any of the other pilots made it back.

Gadara and Torren were at the table, alone. "How did it go today?" Tremol asked Torren.

"We were assigned to Antarctica. There were a lot of alien ships trying to get to the portals," Torren said.

"We spent the day blowing up portals," Gadara added. "How about you two?"

"We spent the day on the East Coast shuttling children to the Med Beds on the Concordance," Keely said.

"Children?" Gadara asked.

"Yes, the pilots found children on some of the ships that were taken out. Most of them were alive and we brought them here to use the Med Beds," Keely said.

"Yes, until we got a call to search for Eno," Tremol said.

"Eno's missing?" Torren asked.

"Yes, and so is his ship."

The White House

Two cloaked ships landed on the roof of the White House after taking out all the reptilian snipers.

"That's a lot of reptiles," Adam said. He and Genesis hovered over the roof, waiting for orders. They were using the night vision capabilities on the Nav-U-Comm. They watched their monitors as the two teams headed down from the roof to take out all the reptiles, using their beam weapons, which were quieter than the laser weapons and had a bigger barrel. But the team also had their laser pistols just in case. All they could see on the monitors was a very small heat signature from each person. The cloaking worked. Their transporter was also cloaked in case the reptiles had any choppers around.

From their vantage point, Adam could see the White House lighting up in different rooms. The whole place had been dark before.

A good thirty minutes later, Adam got the call. "Transporter Two, this is Secure Team One. You're good to land in back of the house."

Adam and Genesis landed the transporter on the back lawn and then everything lit up.

"There!" He pointed. He could see a group of people coming toward them, in a line.

Genesis got to the ramp to let them in. "It looks like a little more than we can carry, Adam."

"We'll take the last few to their vehicles. These people live here," The Secret Service agent said. "You've got the President, his bodyguards, and the few dignitaries that are going back to your system."

"Thank you, sir," Adam said.

"We need all of you to use your seat harnesses," Genesis said. She helped a few people who had trouble adjusting them. When everyone was secured, they headed to the Concordance.

Mercy, New Mexico

Willow Tree sat on the back porch with Eno, gazing at the stars. He tried to show her where he came from, but she just couldn't get what he pointed at.

"Tell me about your system," she said.

"We call our sun Vaedra, and we have nine planets."

"So do we. At least I think so. They've changed the status of Pluto a few times."

"Well, all our planets are habitable except Semtron, because it's too close to Vaedra."

"Oh, yes. We have Mercury, but I don't know much about our other planets."

"I'm from Chroma and we have six moons. Only one has been explored and named. Everyone who lives on Chroma has blond hair and blue eyes, like me."

"Everyone?"

"Yes. Each of our planets was separated by race. At one time, hundreds of anos ago, we all lived on Vestra. They sent out explorers so see which planets were habitable. When they came back, each race was given their own planet so that we could keep the races pure."

"Really? They separated you all by race?"

"Yes. When we were on Vestra, if someone took a mate from a different race, they were exiled to an island. When there were enough people on the island, they brought them here to Earth to live."

"You mean they never saw their families again? Just because they fell in love with someone of the wrong race?"

"Yes. Recently, though, our Councilors brought forth a proposal to end the edict so that we may choose whomever we want to be our mate, no matter what race they are," Eno said.

"Nice."

"Now we can take a mate and live where we choose."

"That's how it is on Earth, but some people give you a hard time if you are mixed, especially the kids. I think people are finally accepting it, though. It's just taken a long time."

"We are all humans, no matter what color we are," Eno said.

"Exactly." She glanced at the stars and then back to Eno. "Is everyone on Chroma as tall as you?"

"We are a tall race, most of us are at least six feet tall. I'm six foot seven inches."

"I thought so. I'm six foot and I haven't met anyone taller than me in a long time."

"There are a lot of people over six foot on the Concordance, but not as tall as me," Eno said.

Willow Tree yawned. "I guess it's time for bed. I'll show you to your room. We'll have to be up early tomorrow since I work 7:00 a.m. until 3:00 p.m."

Willow Tree showed Eno the bedroom and pulled out a

fresh toothbrush for him. "Since this is our guest room, we keep a spare new toothbrush for unexpected company."

He touched her hand when she handed him the toothbrush, and a tingling feeling ran through her.

"You've been more than kind. Thank you." He smiled.

She had a hard time sleeping with thoughts of Eno, running through her head.

Eno lay awake in this strange place, thinking of the events that lead to this moment. The one thing he kept playing over in his mind was seeing the tall, darkly tanned beauty with the long, black braid and brown eyes, holding a spaceship with her mind. He wondered what other gifts she had.

Early Morning, Mercy, New Mexico

"The UFO is still there!" Willow Tree said. She pulled over to the side of the road.

"Why wouldn't it be?" Eno asked. He sat beside her in the front seat.

"Well, after Roswell, the government is usually right there to pick up the pieces. But I guess I forgot to tell them about this."

"Is that bad?"

"I hope I don't get into trouble for it. I'll let the Chief know when we get to the station. He can make that decision."

Willow Tree and Eno exited the vehicle and searched the area for the transponder. After twenty minutes, Willow Tree spotted a black object and picked it up.

"Eno? Is this your transponder?"

"Yes!" He took it from her to examine it. "The signal is gone. It must have been damaged."

"Here are some fragments," she said. She bent down to pick them up.

"It must be what's left of my modulator."

"I'm sorry, Eno. How can I help you contact your people?" She touched his shoulder and felt him tense up.

"I may have to go the military route, but I'm not sure who we can trust down here."

"Come with me to the office. Maybe the Chief can help us out."

"How can he help?"

"Well, he will probably call the military to clean up this mess. When they come out here, maybe they can help you."

"Come on." Willow Tree gently pulled him along. His biceps were firm and big. With his strange-looking flight suit, his build was hidden, except for his broad shoulders.

They rode to the station.

"The Chief wants to see you," Carmela said.

"Wait here," she pointed to her desk. Eno sat at the chair next to the desk as she walked to the Chief's office.

"Yes, sir? You wanted to see me?"

"Have a seat, Moon."

This didn't sound good, she thought, as she sat down across from the Chief's desk.

"What is this report? Are you telling me you fought some aliens to retrieve the girls? Do you know how absurd that sounds?"

"It may sound absurd but it's true."

"Rewrite it!" He threw the report at her.

She caught the papers as they fell. "And how do you want me to write it? Make up something that didn't happen?"

"Try leaving out the aliens and UFO."

"Well then, it would be a lie. I don't do lies."

"Rewrite the damn report and leave out the sci-fi."

"Yes, sir. What happened to my last report?"

"What report?"

"The report on the missing girls."

"You didn't turn in a report."

She glared at him. She knew the truth. What was going on here? She left the office with overwhelming anger building up. Out in the hall, she clenched her fists and took several deep breaths, exhaling slowly. She had to calm down. She refused to take on all his negativity. She marched over to her desk and grabbed Eno's arm.

"Come on." She pulled him up out of his seat. She pulled him into the file room. No one was there.

"What's going on?" Eno asked.

"My report about the missing girls is missing. I'm going to look through the open cases. Something isn't right."

He stood beside her while she looked through the file. She found what she was looking for. Open Cases. She thumbed through those. There were several folders of missing persons, but nothing on the two little girls. Luckily, she still had her copy. She pulled all the open cases out and closed the file cabinet.

"Let's go."

Eno followed her out to her vehicle.

"Get in, we're going rogue today."

"I like the sound of that."

She drove back to the highway where Eno had shot down the UFO, parking alongside the road. She rolled down her windows. "You look through these folders and I'll do this pile."

"What are we looking for?" Eno asked.

"I'm looking for a pattern or a reason these people disappeared. Here, use this." She handed him a pad and pencil from her clipboard tray. She always carried extra. She took one out for herself.

"Why don't we do this in your office?" Eno asked.

"Because my Chief of Police just asked me to write a lie about what happened. And then he said I didn't turn in my other report about the two missing girls, which I handed him yesterday."

"That does sound strange."

"Yes. We're going to get to the bottom of this."

They sat there for almost an hour going through the folders and taking notes when a car going the opposite direction, pulled to a stop across from them. The driver rolled down his window.

"Hello, Mayor Rey," she said. She got a sudden bad feeling.

"Is everything okay, Officer Moon?"

"Yes, everything is fine," she said.

"Who do you have with you, Officer Moon?"

The mayor gave her the creeps. Besides, it was none of his business.

"He's assisting me in a report," she said. Technically, it was sort of true.

"Is he a new officer?" the mayor persisted.

"No. He's not." She wished he would just leave.

"Who is it, then?"

"He's just passing through town. No one you know."

"I can talk to him, if you want me to," Eno said.

She glanced at Eno. "He's being very nosey. And he's up to something," she whispered.

She heard his car engine stop and the door open.

MERCY, NEW MEXICO

"What the hell is that?" the mayor shouted. He glanced over the top of her patrol vehicle. She tried to get out, but he blocked her exit with his body. He bent down really close to her face. "Call the Chief of Police right now. Get him here to deal with this problem before it gets out on the news."

"He knows about the UFO. That's why we're working on the report. He told me to change the report."

The mayor moved around her vehicle and walked toward the UFO. She exited her vehicle and Eno joined her.

"I wouldn't go in there, if I were you," Eno said.

The mayor turned, his brows furrowed, and glared at Eno. "I'll do whatever I damn well please." The mayor continued to the ship.

She ran toward the ship and Eno beat her to it.

"Ugh! What is that foul smell?"

"My guess is it's the rotting corpses of two grey aliens," she said. She put her hands on her hips. Even if this guy was the mayor, he had no business butting into her business.

He turned toward her, his brows still furrowed and glared

at her. "Take care of this mess right now or I can have you fired."

Really? For what reason? "Yes, sir," she saluted him sarcastically. She watched as the mayor stomped off.

"I guess I better call the military," she said.

"Why? Won't your Chief of Police want to do that?" Eno said.

"I thought so, but he told me to leave out the sci-fi in my report. He obviously doesn't believe me or he would have done that already."

She watched the mayor drive off while she headed to the vehicle.

"Willow Tree!" Eno shouted.

She turned to see another UFO above them. This one was shaped like a fat cigar.

"It's one of our transporters!" Eno waved to the ship, which slowly set down nearby.

She glanced around to make sure the mayor was nowhere in sight. Thank goodness, he was gone.

A ramp went down and two humans came out of the ship. She walked back to Eno.

Eno grabbed her arm and pulled her toward him. His grip was firm, but gentle. "These are members of our team," he whispered.

"Eno! Boy, are we glad to see you!" Tremol said.

"We've been trying to reach you," Keely said.

"It's a long story. This is Officer Willow Tree Moon. She helped me take down the greys and we found two little girls they had abducted."

"Are you the team that can take us to the Med Beds?" Willow Tree asked.

"Yes! Are the girls all right?" Keely asked.

"They seem fine, but we were concerned about the implants," Willow Tree said.

"How soon can you get them here?" Tremol asked.

"I can ride out to pick them up. Maybe an hour?"

"Good. You pick up the girls and bring them here while Eno fills us in on what's been happening," Tremol said.

She headed back to her vehicle, a little saddened that Eno was not with her. He had been growing on her. She liked his company, too. At least he knew the truth about what happened. And she still had to deal with the UFO.

She put all the folders into her clipboard, cramming it shut. She would work on that later. She turned her vehicle around and headed into town. She called Mrs. Gonzalez from her phone.

"Hi, Mrs. Gonzalez? This is Officer Willow Tree Moon. I've got us a ride to the Med Beds. Can you call Mrs. Taylor and be ready in 30 minutes?"

"Yes! Yes! We will be ready."

Concordance

"Thank you for your hospitality, Admiral Esrith," the President said.

"I'm glad we could accommodate most of you and I'm sure those on the Reliance will be just as pleased. If you need to go to the Reliance or Endeavor for meetings, we can get you there through our portal system. It's on the bridge section. Just let me know." Esrith handed the President a communicator and another object. "We can keep in touch with this."

"And what is this?"

"That's a sprayer. Squeeze this onto their skin and you'll know immediately if they are human or reptilian."

"Thank you, Admiral. I would like to have a meeting with my Joint Chiefs of Staff. Can you get them all here this afternoon?" the President asked.

"My pleasure. I'll contact you when they are all here, sir." Esrith saluted the President and headed for the bridge.

"Admiral! We just got word about Shadow One," the Ensign said.

"Let's have it."

"Shadow One suffered damage to the communications modulator and the transponder. Eno is fine, but the repairs have to be made on board the Concordance. In the meantime, he's been given Captain Tremol's communicator so he can contact you."

"That's wonderful news!" He let out a sigh of relief and a big smile as he clenched his fists in excitement.

Mescalero Apache Indian Reservation

Eno knocked on the door and Yellow Elk Moon opened it.

"Eno! So good to see you again. Come in!" She glanced past him to see no one there. "How did you get here? Where's Willow Tree?"

"She went to pick up the little girls who were abducted so we can get them to the Med Beds."

"Did you find what you were looking for this morning?"

"Yes, but it was broken. My team showed up and brought me here in their ship. I came to get my ship. I didn't want to just show up and take it without letting you know."

"That was very considerate of you. Thank you. Can I see what it looks like again?"

"Sure." He pressed a button on his device and Shadow One was de-cloaked.

"Oh my, I really like that ship. I could get used to seeing that every day."

"Really?" He scratched his head.

"At night, I've seen many strange things. I've always figured our military was back-engineering ships for themselves. They just didn't admit it."

"Well, maybe it will all come out soon." He patted her shoulder. "There's my team's ship." He pointed up to the sky.

"And that's another shape."

"We call those transporters because we can transport people or things in them. Well, I will see you later."

Eno headed to Shadow One. Using the borrowed communicator, he let Transporter Three know he was ready to go. When he pulled up, he followed Transporter Three to the UFO site.

"Shadow One, this is Transporter Three, can you read?"

"Loud and clear. Go ahead."

"Just wanted to let you know we contacted the Joint Chiefs of Staff via the Reliance and they are sending out the white hats of the military to take care of the UFO."

"Are we still meeting at that spot?"

"Yes. See you in a few," Transporter Three, out."

It was more than a few minutes, but when he arrived, the U.S. Military arrived at the same time.

They all had weapons aimed at him, Tremol, and Keely.

"I'm Captain Tremol from the Concordance. I called this in."

"Weapons down!" A man in a highly decorated unicrin walked forward. "I'm Captain Richard Moon. We're here to take possession of this UFO."

He looked similar to Willow Tree. "Excuse me sir, but are

you related to Willow Tree Moon?"

"Why, yes. Why do you ask?"

"She will be meeting us here shortly. She helped me take down this ship," Eno said.

"She helped you? And how did she do that?"

"Telekinesis."

"Ah, yes. She does have that gift." He turned toward his men. "Come on, men. Let's get this thing loaded."

He didn't explain how he was related. Hmmm. Could they be mates? If so, why didn't he come home last night?

"Sir, there is something you need to see." Eno approached Captain Moon.

"And what is that?"

"I'll show you." He stepped carefully over the dead aliens and went into the ship. He waited for the captain to join him. Behind Captain Moon were Tremol and Keely. He turned toward the center console and pushed a couple buttons and the floor moved down, along with the console. What they stared at were canisters of liquid holding human body parts, all around the ship.

"Those little girls we rescued could have ended up here."

He moved to a wall that had no canister and pressed a button. Inside was a table with a bowl holding intestines and a couple of arms with bite marks on them.

"Oh my gosh!" Keely said. She held her nose from the smell. "I thought the smell was bad outside, but this is worse."

"These greys were hybrids. I checked their mouths. They had sharp teeth. Most greys don't eat human flesh."

"Thank you…"

"Lieutenant Eno ni Esrith, sir." He saluted the captain.

"Thank you, Lieutenant. That will be all."

Eno turned to leave with Tremol and Keely. "Sir, are you

coming up with us?"

"Yes. Yes, I am." Captain Moon joined them and they all left the UFO. When he was out in the open, he saw Willow Tree pull up on the side of the road and another car pulled up behind her. The military had pulled onto the dirt to load up the ship and the aliens.

Willow Tree was followed by the two little girls and both parents of each girl.

"Willow Tree, I forgot to introduce you to part of my team. This is Captain Tremol and his mate, Keely. They are transporting the family to the Med Beds."

"Oh, nice to know your names," she said. She reached out to shake both their hands.

Eno watched Tremol and Keely load up the family in their transporter.

"Aren't you coming, Officer Moon?" Mrs. Taylor asked.

Before she could answer, he spoke. "She's coming with me. We will meet you on the Concordance." He glanced at her and smiled. She smiled back.

"Can I get my radio?" she asked.

"Sure."

When she got back to her vehicle, she grabbed her radio and her clipboard with the folders in it, then locked the car. She ran back to catch up to him.

"Thanks for inviting me. This will be my first ride on a space ship."

"Willow Tree!" Captain Moon called out.

She turned and ran to the man. They embraced awkwardly, since she held her clipboard in one hand. They talked a few minutes and she returned.

Eno led the way to Shadow One. He felt saddened at what he saw. Maybe he was her mate. He had no business spending time with her if she was. He needed to know.

"Before I let you in this ship, tell me. Is Captain Moon your mate?"

"My what?"

"Your mate?"

She laughed. Then she took his arm, pulling him close.

"He's my cousin. His father and my father are brothers."

"Oh. That's good. I did not want to spend time with you if he was your mate."

"Of course not! I would have told you if I was married."

"Married? That's like a mate, right?"

"Yes."

Police Station, Mercy, New Mexico

"Why haven't you taken care of that UFO in the desert?" Mayor Rey said. "Who knows what was on that thing?"

"I thought she made it up. It sounded ludicrous," the Chief said.

"Well, she was out there working on a report you told her to change. So apparently, she didn't make it up."

"She did an investigation of two missing girls," the Chief said.

"We can't have her doing that. You need to stop this investigation now."

"Well her report said she found them on the UFO."

"What were they doing there?"

"The greys must have abducted them."

"They aren't supposed to be doing that in this area."

"What if they were rogue greys?"

"No. That's not possible. They work for the highest bidder and we pay them well. They wouldn't dare cross us."

. . .

Shadow One

"Shadow One to Concordance, come in."

"Glad to hear your voice, Shadow One. Go ahead."

"I'm approaching the landing bay. Permission to land?"

"Permission granted."

A few minutes later, Eno and Willow Tree exited the ship. A tech specialist approached. "We'll get right on that problem, sir."

"Thanks!" He reached his arm out to Willow Tree. "Come with me. I'll give you a tour."

Willow Tree clung to her clipboard in one hand and held on to Eno's arm with the other. She didn't know why she brought the clipboard, except her intuition told her to keep it close. Calling the dispatcher before they left was just a courtesy to let her know she wouldn't be on the radio for a while, but things were usually quiet in Mercy. So quiet that some officers were caught falling asleep in their vehicles.

"This is our flight deck and over there are the tech specialists," Eno said.

She was actually on a space ship! Is this how her ancestors traveled to Earth centuries ago? She glanced around at all the scenery and technology. It was incredible. The whole time she let her mind wander at what she saw, she had forgotten that Eno was explaining things to her.

"What do you say?" Eno looked at her.

"Uh, I'm sorry. I was daydreaming about this wonderful ship. What was the question?"

"Are you hungry?"

"Yes, definitely." She realized she hadn't eaten since breakfast. She glanced at her watch. It was after 4:00 p.m.

She was off the clock, but hadn't done much work today. At least for the City of Mercy.

A door opened. She realized she had been on a super-fast elevator of some sort.

"This is the Med Center. We'll check on the girls and then go to the eating hall and get something to eat," he said.

"Sounds like a plan."

There in front of them were Captain Tremol and Keely, standing with the families.

"Have they taken the girls in, yet?" Eno asked.

"Yes. They found an implant in each of them," Keely said.

"Right now, they are in surgery. Keely and I will arrange for the parents to remain here tonight so we can return them all home tomorrow," Captain Tremol said. Tremol and Keely left.

The parents were sitting in the waiting area, waiting.

"How are you all holding up?" Willow Tree had let go of Eno's arm.

"We're fine," Mrs. Gonzalez said.

"Yes, I'll be glad when it's over," Mr. Taylor said.

"Can we get you anything?" Willow Tree asked.

"No thanks," Mrs. Taylor said. "The healer brought us some drinks a while ago. And we know where the bathrooms are."

"Great. You have my number if you need me. I just don't know if my phone will work up here," she said.

"Let anyone here know you want to talk to Officer Moon, and they can get in touch with me, Eno. I have a communicator that works now." He pointed to his shoulder.

"Thank you," Mrs. Gonzalez said.

He turned to leave and reached for Willow Tree's hand.

His hand was warm, large, and strong. She liked that and glanced up at him.

"I don't want to lose you," he whispered. "Come on, we'll get some food."

When they entered the eating hall, it appeared like a big cafeteria. "It's not as crowded at this time," Eno said.

He helped her with her tray, since she had the clipboard tucked under her arm. "This all looks good," she said. She followed him to some seats and sat down beside him. "So, what happens now?" she asked.

"After we eat, we can work on your report. After that, I'll take you home."

Home? Going home would feel strange after having a taste of this life. "This reminds me of when I was in the military."

"You were?"

"Yes, in the Army, like my cousin. Though we never worked together, I joined because he inspired me."

"Are you still in the military?"

"No. I got out a year ago, but I guess they could still recall me. I joined right out of high school."

"How long is your service?"

"When you join, it's four years."

"Do you ever think of going back?" Eno asked.

"Not really. I wanted to do something else with my life beside drive a Striker."

"What is that?"

"A large vehicle for hauling people."

"Oh, like a transporter."

"Well, our vehicles don't fly."

"Would you like to learn?"

"Sure!"

"First let's work on that report."

❧ 10 ❧
CONCORDANCE

Eno finished giving her the tour of the ship.

"This seems like an awesome ship. Are you enjoying your service here?" she asked.

"Yes. I'll have to show you my quarters. I have one of the biggest rooms on the ship."

"Wow."

"Here's where all the officers hang out," Eno said.

The door hissed open to what looked like a large bar area with plenty of tables, but more lighting than you'd find in a bar on Earth.

"Eno! Come join us," a woman called out.

"That's Captain Gadara. She taught all of us how to fly."

Willow Tree walked to the table with Eno, her clipboard tucked under her arm.

"Everyone, this is Willow Tree Moon, a police officer for the town of—"

"Mercy, New Mexico," she finished.

"Welcome aboard the Concordance," Captain Gadara said.

"The captain is mate to Torren Conley," Eno pointed to him.

"Nice to meet you both."

Two others walked over to the table.

"Have a seat," Captain Gadara said. Eno pulled out a chair for her, then sat beside her.

"Another law enforcement person," a familiar red-haired woman said.

"You already know Keely and her mate, Captain Tremol," Eno said.

"I'm with Secret Service and Tremol is with the Inter-planetary Space Patrol. We're the new liaisons for the dignitary exchange we have going on between Earth and the Vaedra system."

"Oh, yes. I remember the President mentioned that at one time."

"What have you got there?" Keely asked.

"I worked on a report the other day about the disappearance of two little girls. Then I did a follow-up report. The Chief of Police asked me to rewrite the second report and leave out the sci-fi and my first report disappeared."

"We were working on it when a hostile man interrupted us," Eno said.

She glanced at him. "He *was* hostile, wasn't he?"

Eno nodded. "He ordered her around."

"Who was he?" Captain Tremol asked.

"The mayor of Mercy. I'm not particularly fond of him."

She opened her clipboard. "I pulled all the open files out and brought them with me so I could search for my report. What we started to find before we were interrupted was there were a lot of missing children from Mercy."

"Really? Is it a small town?" Keely asked.

"Yes. And it's rural so it's spread out. I've lived near there all my life and don't remember hearing about any of these missing children."

"What's the time frame?" Keely asked.

"I think the oldest was five years ago," Eno added.

"I started to take notes of things that stood out to see if there was a pattern," she said.

"Were any of them abducted by aliens?" Torren asked.

"Not that I know of, but I wouldn't have known that the two little girls were abducted by aliens if I hadn't gone door to door asking the neighbors if they had seen anything."

"Someone saw that?" Keely asked.

"Not the abduction, but a neighbor had seen a UFO hovering in the neighborhood and called it in. My dispatcher thought it was a joke and didn't report it to me, while I was there in the neighborhood."

"Incompetent fool. He should be fired!" Captain Tremol said.

"Unfortunately, he is a she and the niece of the Chief of Police. I don't see that happening."

"On these other cases, did the officer go door to door asking questions?" Keely asked.

"No. They were all done by the only detective we have. He just wrote down what the parents told him and that was it."

"Maybe we could go back and do that," Eno said.

"You mean, follow up on all these cases?"

"Sure. I'll help you." He touched her hand.

"What about your responsibilities here? I wouldn't want you to get into trouble."

"I volunteered for this mission, so I can un-volunteer," Eno said.

Captain Gadara laughed. Hard.

"I'd like to see you try that," Torren said.

"I have that sector to watch for the greys' ships. I can help her and watch the skies at the same time," Eno said.

"I appreciate your help, Eno. I don't think I will get help from my own department. Something about this just doesn't feel right."

"If we can help you, Willow Tree, let us know," Keely said.

"I'll see if we can get you a communicator," Captain Tremol said.

"I have one," Eno said.

"You have mine. I need to get both of you one," Captain Tremol said.

"Did they get your ship fixed yet?" Keely asked.

"They are working on it now."

Captain Gadara and Torren, Keely and Captain Tremol all looked over toward the entrance. She turned to see who it was.

Eno whispered, "That's Adam and Genesis."

The two of them joined the group at the table.

"There's a hell of a battle going on in Washington, DC," Adam said.

"What's happening?" Torren asked.

"Damn reptilians everywhere. It's like the place is infested with them."

"My parents are staying at my place in D.C.," Keely said.

"A lot of people are evacuating the area," Genesis said.

"I think they're getting ready to blow the place up," Adam said.

"Washington?" Torren asked.

"We spent the day moving white hats out of the area."

"We also brought back the bodies of the fallen," Genesis added.

"The fallen?" Torren asked.

"We lost six security people who were with the CMOs," Genesis said.

"The Admiral is preparing a ceremony for them this afternoon," Adam said.

"What happened to them?" Gadara asked.

"They were killed by the reptilians."

Eno stood. "We need to get her report done."

"I just looked at it," Keely said. "I don't see anything wrong with it."

Willow Tree stood beside Eno, gathering her folders. "The Chief wants me to remove the sci-fi."

"If you do that, it won't be a true report," Keely said.

"Exactly."

"If you go over the Chief's head, who would that be?" Captain Tremol asked.

"The mayor. I don't trust him either."

"Who else could you go to?" Captain Tremol asked.

"Well, the FBI has been compromised, so I guess my senator. But with all that's happening right now, I don't trust any of them."

"You're on your own, then," Captain Gadara said.

"No, she's not. She's got us," Torren said. "We stick together. If she's a friend of Eno's, she a friend to us."

"Thank you. Thank you all." She felt hopeful as Eno led her out of the Lounge.

"Where are we going?" she asked.

"I'll show you my quarters. We can finish the work there."

"This is nice," she said when they entered his quarters.

"Have a seat," Eno said.

"Oh, you mean the only one in the room?"

"Of course." Eno sat on the bed and opened her clipboard.

He read over the report. "And what is the problem with this report?"

"I need to remove the sci-fi, so basically everything about the UFO and the aliens and finding the girls in the ship."

"Keely is right. You should leave this as is. It's what happened. I can sign it as a witness. Your cousin can also sign it as a witness after the fact."

"That's right. Thank you, Eno."

He took a pen and signed his name at the bottom of the report. "Now, let's make a list of where we will start tomorrow."

"Good idea." She wrote down the addresses and the names involved, along with their phone numbers. All the missing children were from different neighborhoods, so she organized a list of those.

"So, you're really going to help me do this tomorrow?" she asked.

He nodded. "You know what I've been meaning to ask you," Eno said.

"No?" Her heart pounded. Where was he going with this?

"What type of weapon are you wearing?"

"It's a Sig Sauer." She stood and pulled it out, removed the clip and handed him her weapon.

"That's heavier than our stunners."

"What's a stunner?"

"It can knock someone unconscious for several minutes or hours, depending on how many times you hit them. We don't try to kill anyone, but if we have to, we use full stun and hit them twice. Except the reptilians. Two hits at full stun will only knock them out."

"Well, mine is meant to kill, so we don't pull it out unless we have to." She moved closer and touched his arm. "You know what I've been meaning to ask *you*?" She glanced up into his pale blue eyes.

"What?" His brows raised in anticipation. He smiled and locked onto her eyes. She almost forgot her question, his gaze was so intense and distracting.

"Can I have one of those weapons you took from the greys?"

"Ha! A woman after my own heart." He gathered up her clipboard and helped her pack her folders. He took her hand and led her to the stairs. One flight down and they were on the flight deck. He spoke with a systems tech about his ship.

"It's ready," he said. "It's over here." He walked her to Shadow One and within a minute, they were walking up the ramp. After they both entered the ship, he walked to the back and unlocked a compartment behind the seats.

"I stored them back here." He pulled one of the weapons out.

"These are dangerous. We'll try some target practice tomorrow." He handed it to her and she held it in her arms.

"This is heavy, but not as heavy as my military rifle was." She handed it back to him. "I can't wait to try it out tomorrow."

"Me, too." He locked up the weapon and they both sat in their seats while he did pre-flight. He noticed she watched every move, so he explained what he did.

"I'm a fast learner, so I appreciate you explaining things."

"Here we go. Shadow One to Command Center," he said.

"Go ahead, Shadow One."

"Permission to exit the Concordance."

"Permission granted."

He explained a lot of things he did while they flew back to the reservation, and she took it all in.

Once they were over New Mexico, she called her parents on her cell phone.

"Willow Tree, the Chief of Police was here looking for you," her mother said. She was probably in deep trouble.

"I'll call him, Mom. I just wanted to let you know I was all right and I'll be home shortly."

"I saved you some dinner. Is Eno coming with you?"

"Yes, he is."

"Good. I have enough food for both of you. I hope you are hungry."

"I sure am. Love you, Mom."

"Love you, too."

"I take it someone is looking for you?" Eno asked.

"Yes. The Chief of Police. I need to call him." She dialed his number.

"Where the hell have you been? We tried to contact you on the radio with no response."

"I'm sorry, Chief. I accompanied the two little girls who were abducted, along with their parents, to the Med Beds on the Concordance."

"I told you to drop that shit off your report."

"That wasn't on the report, sir. It happened after the fact."

"You're done with those people. All you needed to do was jot down the basic information. That's all. I don't want you spending any more time on those people. You're not a babysitter, you got that? We have an investigator and that's his job."

"Yes sir."

"Report to me first thing in the morning. I have a new assignment for you."

"Yes sir."

Eno had the ship cloaked since they were in Earth's atmosphere. He lowered his craft into the back yard of

Willow Tree's parents' home. She dreaded what lay ahead of her. What could the Chief possibly mean by a new assignment?

"I take it your Chief just changed our plans?"

"I think so. We'll see in the morning." Disappointment flowed over her.

Eno leaned close to her and lifted her chin.

"I guess we'll have to wake earlier than usual to get some target practice in, won't we?" He winked.

"Yes, we will." She smiled. She couldn't wait to get her hands on one of those weapons.

MESCALERO APACHE INDIAN RESERVATION

Early the next morning, after breakfast, Willow Tree and Eno took a few shots at some large boulders on the back of her parents' property. It was still dark outside.

With the press of the trigger, the large boulder evaporated with only a small hissing sound.

"Oh my gosh!"

"I hope you weren't fond of that rock," Eno said.

"Not at all." She fired again at several different boulders and they were gone.

Eno tried his weapon and did the same thing.

"Let's try this button," he said. He pointed to a button on the side of the weapon. The hissing sound was softer, but instead of evaporating the boulder, it melted the center of it.

"What the hell?" she said. She walked over to the boulder and touched it. The rock was cold. "It's like it melted the rock. It's smooth all inside it with no particles around the bottom."

"Go ahead and finish it off," he said.

She pushed the button and tried the trigger again. Now,

she had two rocks. She pushed the button again and pulled the trigger, evaporating both rocks with one shot.

"Awesome! Can I have this? Please?"

He put his arm around her, pulling her close. "Since you asked nicely, you sure can. Just don't tell anyone because I haven't reported this yet." He kissed her forehead.

"It's our secret." She rose on her toes and kissed his cheek.

She put her weapon in the back of her patrol vehicle, while Eno returned his to his ship.

"I'm heading in to work, Eno. I'll keep you posted on what the Chief has to say," she spoke into her new communicator, she wore as a wristband.

"I'll hover over the skies of Mercy and then the rest of New Mexico, waiting to hear from you," he said.

Mercy Police Station

By the time she got to the Police Station, just the dispatcher was there. The Chief usually didn't come in until 8:00 am.

"Hello Carmela," she said, trying to be nice.

"Someone's in trouble," Carmela sang.

"What are you talking about?" She clutched her clipboard. She would have to return those files before the Chief came in.

"All that nonsense about a UFO the other day. The Chief called the military to pick it up and there was nothing there."

"The Chief called the military?" Willow Tree asked.

"Oh, he's very upset about it. The ordeal made him look bad so he's quite pissed at you."

"Well, the military *did* pick it up way before that. I took care of it." She walked to her desk and called her cousin on her cell phone.

"Richard?"

"Willow Tree! How are you?"

"I'm good. My Chief of Police called the military yesterday to pick up the UFO in the desert. Of course they couldn't find it, but I was wondering why they didn't know it was already picked up?"

"Oh, that must have been the black hats. They don't know what we're doing and we need to keep it that way."

"I'm in trouble for it because the Chief thinks I made everything up."

"I'm sorry Willow Tree, but you may have to take the heat for a while until everything is clear to go."

"What does that mean?"

"I can't tell you, but everything will come to light soon."

"Thanks."

Now what? She stood and pulled out the folders from her clipboard. She went over each file to make sure she had all the information she needed to check on the families this afternoon.

"Carmela, I'm going to make my rounds and be back before the Chief gets here."

Carmela sat filing her nails. "We'll see you then, I guess."

She drove in toward town and made her way through, slowly, to make sure everything seemed fine as usual. Then headed back to the station. When she pulled in to the parking lot, the Chief was not there, so she pulled her list out and made her first call.

"Mrs. Morris?"

"You've got the wrong number. I've had this number for five years."

"Oh, I'm very sorry." She hung up and glanced at her list

and the number she just called on the phone. It was the same number. She made notes about what just happened, then headed inside.

She walked to her desk and sat down, checking her list. Before she could call the second person, the Chief of Police came in, followed by the mayor.

Great.

"Inside my office, Moon. Now," he barked.

Wow. This doesn't look good. At all.

She went inside and noticed the mayor stood beside the Chief of Police.

"Close the door, Moon," he ordered.

She did, then turned around. "Yes, sir?"

"What do you actually do all day, Moon?" the mayor asked.

"Sir, is this a conversation between you and me, or is the mayor allowed to question me as well?"

"Answer the damn question, Moon," the Chief said.

"I patrol the downtown area, the rural highway, the country roads, I talk to the people, making sure everything is working well."

"Have you ever napped on the job?" the mayor asked.

"No sir, you have me confused with the second or third shift."

"Moon! What the hell happened to you yesterday?" the Chief asked.

"I was out of radio contact because I was off the planet."

"Off the planet?" the mayor asked.

She looked at the Chief instead of the mayor. He was creeping her out to say the least. And why was he even here?

"I asked you a question!" The mayor raised his voice.

"I explained it to the Chief of Police already, Mayor."

"Well you can explain it to me now!" the mayor raised his

voice again.

"I accompanied the two children that were abducted by aliens to the Concordance, along with their parents, to have the implants removed."

"Oh, so you have a UFO of your own now?"

"No sir, but I did get a ride with a pilot who does have his own ship."

"That's it, Moon! You're on desk duty the rest of the day and second shift the rest of the week."

Her eyes widened at the sound of her sentence. "Yes, sir. Is that all?" She clenched her jaw. Keep cool. Don't panic. She took in a deep breath. Boot camp was much worse.

"I want that report now."

"It's on my desk, sir."

"Well, get it!" he shouted.

She turned and left the office. It felt like she was in the Army all over again.

She pulled the report out of her clipboard and hurriedly made copies. She dropped the copies off on her desk and brought the Chief the originals.

"You didn't make the changes?"

"No sir, because what is on the report is what happened."

"Who is this Eno?"

"A witness."

"You didn't say there were any witnesses."

"It's in the report, sir."

"You better change it now, Moon. I've got reporters who are constantly asking to see the latest reports," the mayor said.

"You mean, lie, mayor?"

"Change the damn report!" the Chief said loudly.

She took the report from him and went back to her desk.

"Eno, come in, this is Willow Tree."

"Go ahead, Willow Tree."

"I'm sorry, but I can't leave the office today. The rest of this week, I'll be on second shift, working 3:00 p.m to 11:00 p.m."

"I'll cover the skies today and I'll see you tonight."

"Thank you."

The thought of seeing him again made her smile, despite her current situation.

She pulled out the copies and made another set of copies, highlighting everything that looked like science fiction, although it pained her to do it. Then she re-typed the whole report, making it look ridiculous without the whole truth. She had an idea. She looked up the local newspaper's email address and the next biggest city's newspaper. Then she photographed the report with her phone and emailed them both copies of the original report with her explanation of why she was sending it.

She went down the list she made with Eno and started calling the people on it. After about an hour with either number not in service or wrong number, she stopped for lunch.

"I'll be back in a bit, Carmela. I'm going out to lunch. Can I pick up anything for you?"

"Why don't you bring me back a UFO burger?" she laughed.

Willow Tree shook her head at Carmela's comment and headed to the café on the edge of town.

Shadow One

Eno flew from New Mexico to California and back with nothing in sight. When everything seemed quiet, he got a call on his communicator.

"Ardent One to anyone in the Dulce, New Mexico, area. I've got several targets trying to escape the area. I can't get them all."

"This is Shadow One, I'm on it," Eno said.

The caller was the pilot from the Reliant. He sent his location to Eno's Nav-U-Com. He was able to find the location quickly and caught a grey ship unawares. He blasted it with his ship's cannon and watched it fall from the sky. Another ship shot out just behind it and he blasted it as well. It wobbled before falling to the ground.

"I got two of them and I'm going after them to take them out," he said.

"I've got this one and another," the Ardent pilot said.

Eno landed near the first ship he hit and pulled out the alien weapon he got from the ship he shot the other day.

He pushed the button to only make an opening in case there were other humans on board. Once he blasted the ship, two greys fell outside. He pushed the button again and evaporated both of them. Climbing on board, he found a couple of cages with humans inside. He pulled his stunner out and shot the lock.

"Are you all able to walk?"

"Yes!" The group crawled out of the short cages and he helped them out of the ship. There were five humans, two males and three females.

"Is there anyone else on board?"

"That was all of us," one of the men said.

"Shadow One to Transporter Three, come in."

"Transporter Three, go ahead."

"I've got five humans who need to be seen by the CMO. Can you pick up?"

"On our way. We got your location. It will be a few minutes."

"Shadow One, out."

"I need to check another ship nearby," he told the group. "Wait here and someone will pick you up for medical checks to remove the implants."

"How did you know they did that?" one of the women asked.

"That's what the greys do to track you. I'll be back shortly."

He climbed back into Shadow One, which was still cloaked, and took off to the last spot he had seen the grey ship. He almost missed it because it blended in with the scenery.

The ramp was down, which meant they might have escaped. He took both the stunner and the alien weapon. But before he left his ship, he took his ship's portable scanner to see if there were any heat signatures.

First, he checked out the grey's ship, making the move up the ramp, the alien weapon ready, but there was no one inside. Not even any humans. He picked up two heat signatures just past the ship and climbed back into Shadow One, moving his ship back into the air. The signatures got stronger the farther away he flew. There they were, running to a hill. He lowered his ship to land near the hill and jumped from his ship with the alien weapon set to destroy. He hit one and then the other, evaporating both of them. He went back to his ship and moved closer to the grey's craft, for one last look. He headed back to the first ship and waited with the small group.

"Ardent One, this is Shadow One, come in."

"Ardent One, go ahead."

I have survivors from the first ship but none from the second. I've got Transporter Three on the way."

"I'm checking mine now," the pilot said.

"Watch out for their blasters," he warned.

"What have you done now Willow Tree?" Kyle Proctor asked.

He was the swing shift person. She would be doing his shift the rest of the week.

"I'm straightening the file room," she said. Her arms were full of the missing children's files. She was really putting back the files she borrowed, but he didn't need to know that.

"I mean what have you done to get switched around like this?"

She motioned for him to follow her. She led him into the file room. Hopefully, she could trust him. He was a police officer, after all, and a former veteran. And if you couldn't trust them, then you had no one.

"I wrote up a report about an incident," she said. She pulled the report out from the stack of folders and handed it to him. While he looked it over, she returned the files she had 'borrowed'.

"Wow. This happened here in Mercy?"

"Yes. The Chief told me to change the report and take out the sci-fi. Then he was mad because he sent the military to pick up the UFO, but the pilot who helped me called that in to his people and the military hauled it off while I was there."

She continued to return files to the drawer.

"Wait, he called the military before or after you saw it hauled off?"

"After. And the military guys that the Chief called were unaware it had already been hauled off."

"That's odd."

"Yes. Apparently there are white hats and black hats in the military."

"What does that mean?"

"The white hats are the good guys and the black hats are the bad guys," she said.

"We have good military and bad military?" Kyle asked. "I don't remember that going on while I was in service."

"Yes. Who would have thought, right? I'd like to think I was a white hat back when I was in the military."

"So, the Chief is punishing you because the military took the UFO?" Kyle asked.

"Yes, plus the mayor came in here asking me all sorts of questions."

"What's Rey doing here, anyway? It's really none of his business, is it?"

"That's what I thought, but he's making it his business now."

She finished putting the files in the drawers.

Kyle handed her the report. "Anything else I need to know about? Anything going on in town?"

"Nothing. Oh, except the parents of the children I recovered left their car parked on the side of the road on Highway 54. Just make sure it's still there."

"Why did they do that?"

"Because the Vaedrans picked them up in their space craft and took them to their Star Destroyer to use the Med Beds."

"Vaedrans? Med Beds? What are you talking about?"

"Didn't you read my report?"

"Well, most of it."

She rolled her eyes at him. Men. She would never understand their thinking process.

"The kids who were abducted by the grey aliens had implants in them, so the greys could track them. The Vaedrans took them to their ship where they could remove the implants."

"Oh, well, when you say it out loud, it does sound a little crazy."

"But it's all true. This really happened."

"Okay. I believe you. What did the Vaedrans look like?"

"They're human. Just like you and me. In fact, one of them was from Earth."

"How do you know, did you have a conversation with them?"

"As a matter of fact, I did. I had a drink with a lot of others from the Vaedra star system. It seems three of them have Earthen mates."

"Earthen what?"

"Mates. You know, like spouses."

"Earthens? You mean like Earthlings?"

"Well, they call us Earthens. That reminds me, I'm supposed to meet with one of their pilots tonight." She glanced at her watch, next to her communicator. "It's almost quitting time for me," she said.

"I would have been here sooner but I had a dentist appointment today. I'm supposed to finish your shift today and then do mine."

"Well, I don't know if a few minutes today counts as

working my shift. Tomorrow, I work your 3 to 11 shift and you work mine, correct?"

"Yes. Then I'm off after that," Kyle said.

"Well, there you go. It was all an inconvenience to teach me a lesson," Willow Tree said.

"I'll let the Chief know I'm here and then I'll do the patrolling."

She watched him walk into the Chief's office. She then continued straightening the files and the file room, killing time until she could go home. She wanted this day to be over.

Kyle waved as he left and she waved back. He was a good guy. Not like Darryl Kline. Darryl was the detective who took down all the reports of missing children. She felt as if he really didn't care about what he did. And after reading his reports, he really didn't get much information. It was as if he didn't even try. Where was he anyway? Shouldn't he have been here today? He was usually always in the office.

Sid Reed was the second shift person, but he was off today and tomorrow, that's why Kyle came in. With Ed Davis, the four of them pretty much were the whole Mercy Police Department, not counting the dispatchers. The Chief never patrolled any more. He was content with doing paperwork, or so he complained.

She glanced at her watch again. Ah, quitting time. After the way her morning started, she looked forward to the end of her shift.

When she got to the patrol car, she called Eno to see how his day had gone, but he didn't respond. Maybe he was in space. She hoped everything was all right. She backed out of her parking spot. When she put the vehicle into drive, there stood the mayor, in front of her car. *Damn. What did he want?* She put the car in park.

He walked toward her window, so she rolled it down.

"You had better watch your step, Officer Moon. I'll be watching you." He turned and walked away.

She rolled up her window. That was certainly a threat. She shuddered at the thought. Putting the vehicle in drive, she headed home. He gave her the creeps, but she didn't know why.

After spending most of the morning making phone calls, she ended up with nothing new. All of the phone numbers of the parents of the missing children were either bogus to start with, or everyone changed their phone numbers. Everyone. Could that be possible? In this small town, where everyone knows your business? All she had left to do was check out the addresses. She wondered if they were actually real, now that the phone numbers didn't jive. Tomorrow, she would find out.

Shadow One

"Shadow One, this is Ardent One, come in."

"Go ahead, Ardent One."

"Thanks for the warning. I got both the aliens, but I took a hit. Need assistance." He sounded winded.

"On my way, Ardent One."

Eno picked up his location from his communications and landed near the alien ship. When he found the pilot, he was unconscious but he had a pulse.

"Shadow One to Transporter Three, come in."

"Transporter Three, go ahead."

"I've got a pilot down, along with some humans that need rescuing."

"We're at the site with the humans. We've got a lock on your location. We will be there shortly."

He quickly checked for any other humans on board the greys' ship. These humans were also in pieces and preserved in liquid-filled glass containers. Why did these creatures insist on experimenting with people? Couldn't they just leave people alone and experiment on their own kind?

By the time the transporter arrived, he had checked the location of injury on the pilot.

"Captain Tremol, he's been hit with a laser in his side, but he managed to kill the two greys," Eno said.

"Any humans on board?"

"Only pieces of them. Much like the first ship I shot down."

"We'll call in the location to the general so he can call in the U.S. Military for pick up," Tremol said.

Keely joined them with a hover gurney and a first aid kit. She wrapped a healing bandage around the pilot's wound. Eno and Captain Tremol lifted the pilot onto the gurney and helped Keely secure him on the transporter for the trip.

"He was a pilot for the Reliance. His ship is Ardent One," he said.

"Got it. We'll take him first since the Reliance is closer. The others will continue on with us to the Concordance," Tremol said.

He stood by and watched the Transporter take off, then waited for the U.S. Military. Since there were three ships down, the military needed several large vehicles to load the ships onto.

When they arrived, he greeted Captain Moon. "Hello Captain Moon, remember me?"

"Yes, Lieutenant Eno, right?"

"Yes sir. We have three ships and one has similar body parts as the first one you picked up," he said.

"Thanks for the warning. By the way, why aren't there any dead aliens here?"

"I shot them to make sure they were dead. The weapon I

used evaporated them. But one ship has two dead aliens beside it," he said. He hoped he didn't ask any more questions because he wasn't planning on giving up his newly acquired weapon.

The captain turned to his men and gave orders. Eno stepped away to give them room to do their work.

He realized how similar Captain Moon's deeply tanned skin resembled Willow Tree's coloring. He liked that about her. His skin was pale and if he stayed out in this hot desert sun too long, he would burn. One of the failings of his people was their ability to burn easily. With time and protective creams, he could tan, but never as dark as Willow Tree and her family. And with his career as a pilot in the Star Force, his chances of seeing the sun were slim, unless he got assignments like this. He actually enjoyed stepping out of the ship and being on land. It had been so long since he had done that. He realized how much he missed it.

When the last ship was secure, he glanced at his chrono. It was past the time for Willow Tree to be off from work. That's when he saw the message light on his communicator. When he pressed it, it showed Willow Tree had called. He must have been on his communicator and missed it. He returned her call.

"Eno?" He liked the sound of her voice. It made him smile.

"Yes, I was busy today and didn't hear your call. How was your day?"

"Not as good as it could have been, but I'll tell you about it later. Are you coming for dinner?"

"Is that your evening meal?" His stomach growled at the thought of food. He realized he hadn't eaten since breakfast with Willow Tree and that had been really early this morning.

"Yes."

"I will be there shortly. Your mother is a wonderful cook." He didn't remember ever having food cooked by his mother. In fact, he remembered being on a ship most of his life and eating the ship's food. At least they ate together, whether or not his mother cooked it. But the few times he visited his father's parents or his mother's parents, he did get a home cooked meal.

"She will be glad to hear it. See you soon."

MESCALERO APACHE INDIAN RESERVATION

Willow Tree helped her mother set the table while they waited for Eno's arrival. She felt a little excited at the thought of seeing him again. The doorbell rang and Bear Hunter went to answer the door. Her heart hitched at the thought of him entering the house. But Eno never used the front door before.

"Willow Tree!" Bear Hunter called out.

"Yes, Dad?" She called while heading to the door.

"Kyle? Is everything all right?" she asked. Her heart jumped at the thought something could be wrong.

"I went down Hwy 54 to check on the vehicle you spoke about."

"Yes?"

"Well, it was there so I walked around it to check it out and a UFO landed nearby in the desert."

"What did it look like?" she asked.

"Like a cigar shape."

"Oh, that was probably the transporter team bringing back the families."

"Yes! Both families came toward me and I asked their names. Gonzalez and Taylor."

"Yes. So what happened after that?"

"They got in their car and drove away."

"So why are you here?"

"I just had to tell somebody. It was just so unbelievable, I had to make sure I didn't imagine it."

"Do you want to see something else just as unbelievable?" Bear Hunter asked.

Kyle shrugged his shoulders. "It depends."

Bear Hunter motioned for Kyle to follow him. She followed both of them. As they walked through the house, she saw Eno step into the dining room.

"Kyle, this is Eno ni Esrith. He's from the Vaedra system," Bear Hunter said.

"Hello," Eno said.

"The Vaedra system?" Kyle asked.

"Yes, it's closer than the Andromeda system," Eno said.

"Show Kyle your ship, Eno," Willow Tree said. She realized she was smiling and excited at the same time.

Watching Kyle follow Bear Hunter and Eno outside, she realized that Kyle was much shorter than all of them.

Eno pressed a device on his wrist and the cloaking disappeared.

"Oh my gosh! So you're an alien?" Kyle asked.

"To your planet, yes, but I'm just as human as you are."

Kyle reached out and shook Eno's hand. "It's nice to meet you."

"Same here," Eno said. He glanced at her and back to Kyle.

"Kyle witnessed the Transporter dropping off the two families today," she said.

"While you are here, Kyle, would you like to eat dinner with us? We're having venison," Yellow Elk said.

"Why, yes, if you're sure you have enough?"

"We have plenty," Yellow Elk said.

This time, she managed to sit beside Eno, with Kyle sitting across from them and her parents across from each other as before. During grace, while she held Eno's hand, he gave her hand a squeeze. A warm feeling rushed through her body and she squeezed his hand back.

After saying grace, Kyle spoke up. "I'm really sorry for interrupting your dinner, but I just had to talk to someone who wouldn't think I was crazy."

"I know exactly how you feel, Kyle," she said. She glanced at Eno and then her parents. "Here, you are safe."

"Other than your transporter experience, did anything else happen today?" Eno asked. He took some meat from the plate and passed the venison to her.

"Well, there was something weird that happened earlier," Kyle said. He glanced at her. "After you left, I came back to the office because I forgot my clipboard and I overheard the Chief talking to Mayor Rey."

"Really? What were they talking about?" she asked.

"I think they were talking about you."

"Explain that," Eno said. He sat up straighter in his seat.

"Well, I heard only parts of the conversation, but it sounded like, 'what are we going to do about *her*?' and 'good police officers are hard to find.'"

"The mayor threatened me this afternoon when I was leaving the parking lot." she said.

"What?" Bear Hunter asked. His brows furrowed.

"Yes. He told me to watch my step because he was watching me."

"I don't like that man," Yellow Elk said.

"Something needs to be done about him," Eno said.

"There's something going on tonight," Kyle said.

"How do you know?" Willow Tree asked.

"Well, the Chief said, 'see you tonight,' when the mayor was leaving."

Ideas rolled around in Willow Tree's head, but she didn't want to say anything while Kyle was there. After dinner, he thanked Yellow Elk for the meal and Willow Tree walked him to the door.

"Be careful, Kyle," she said.

"I will. See you tomorrow."

When she closed the door, she leaned on it.

"It looks like you have an idea," Eno said. "I can see your brain processing something."

She walked toward the table and started picking up the dishes. "Yes. An idea *is* cooking in my brain."

Eno helped her clear the table. She loaded the dishwasher as Eno handed her the plates.

"I need to train you on astral projection, Willow Tree," Bear Hunter said.

"Astral what?" She stood up and glanced at her father. Eno watched him as well.

"When the soul leaves the body."

"You mean like dying?" Willow Tree asked.

"No. Our ancestors used astral projection to search for the enemy. They did that to learn what the enemies' plans were. Your soul comes back to your body."

"You could learn what the Chief is up to," Eno said. He had put his hand on her back.

"I don't know about that," she hesitated. "I don't under-stand how that works. What if something goes wrong?"

"You start with meditating. Use your third eye to project your spirit outward," Bear Hunter explained.

Eno turned her around, putting his hands on both her shoulders and looked her in the eyes. "I'll do it with you."

"You would do that? For me?" Her heart beat harder in her chest.

"Sure. I meditate daily. I just never thought to do the astral projection." His hands were still on her shoulders. The warmth penetrated throughout her body. She swallowed hard.

"All right. After we clean up this kitchen, then I'll do it."

Eno helped her finish the dining room clean-up and then the kitchen. About thirty minutes later, they went into the living room to speak with Bear Hunter.

Bear Hunter moved the furniture around so there was plenty of room on the floor. Then he turned down the lights. "Lie down," he said.

She lay on the floor and Eno lay beside her.

"I think you should do this as well," Yellow Elk said.

"Maybe I should," Bear Hunter said. "You will awaken us if anything happens," he said to Yellow Elk.

Bear Hunter lay on the sofa. He spoke softly, easing them into a meditative state. "You must be in a state of deep relaxation."

Yellow Elk turned on some meditation music. It played softly, while Bear Hunter spoke. "Concentrate on your body and how it feels. You want to be completely relaxed in mind and body. Start with your toes and work your way up to your head."

She sat up and removed her shoes. Eno sat up beside her and did the same thing. She lay back down. She had been meditating since she was a child, so getting into this state was easy for her.

While Bear Hunter spoke, she concentrated on her breathing and using her third eye to 'see' with.

"Feel vibrations and your head clearing. Envision golden,

white light. Let your mind wander to a part of your body, like your hand or foot. Flex your foot in your mind only. Visualize this until it seems real," he said. "Use your mind to move your soul from your body."

She watched herself, lying on the floor next to Eno. She moved through the room and outside. The sky was beautiful, with a full moon. She could see for miles as she flew over the terrain. In a moment, she was downtown. She saw Kyle driving slowly through town, doing his patrol. A motion caught her eye and she saw the Chief getting into a patrol vehicle. She followed him. She was aware of Eno's spirit next to her. The Chief moved farther away from town, near the outskirts before pulling off the road. He drove a ways before parking behind a large boulder. She watched as he exited the vehicle and walked a short distance to another boulder and walked through it.

She followed him. It had been a hologram. How long had that been there? They were in a tunnel, where the Chief got into another vehicle with someone else. She followed them further into the tunnel where it split right and left. They continued right. About a mile in, the vehicle stopped. The Chief got out and the vehicle went back to the entrance.

She was hovering near the top of the tunnel where she could see a large group, gathering together. There must have been over a hundred people. Now, she was aware of a third spirit. Bear Hunter?

"Yes, I am here," she heard in her mind. "I'm going to the left tunnel."

Several of the people in the group wore long black robes. They were chanting and doing some sort of ritual. The incantations sounded demonic. She got a bad vibe from it.

A child was brought into the room, screaming. Someone ripped the child's clothes off. It was a little boy, around seven or eight years old. She didn't recognize him. Then the unthinkable happened. Several of the people in robes, including the mayor, shifted into seven-foot, brownish-green reptiles, the robes falling away.

Then, the one that had been the mayor, slashed the child's throat and the rest of them fought to get a drink of the child's spurting blood. The reptiles crowded around the child, the rest of the group chanting louder. A few minutes went by and the reptiles backed away. There was a shell of what used to be a little child, lying on an altar of sorts.

She felt herself gasp and noticed the mayor glanced up at the ceiling. Did he see her? Could he hear her?

She opened her eyes and she was on the floor of her house.

"What happened?" Willow Tree asked.

"You gasped. What did you see, child?" Yellow Elk asked in a whisper. She reached her hand to her, helping her up off the floor. Yellow Elk guided her into another room.

While she explained what she saw, Eno came awake and then Bear Hunter. They joined the two women in the dining room.

"That was disturbing," Eno said. "I looked away and saw another large group of people, taking turns, raping a woman. I fear she was next."

Bear Hunter rubbed his forehead. "I went to the tunnel on the left. It was full of cages. In each cage was a child or young person. They were dirty and naked. Rows upon rows of cages, with greys walking up and down the aisles."

"We've got to stop this!" she said.

"How? The Chief of Police is involved. The mayor and town officials were all there," Bear Hunter said.

"I know how," Eno said. He tapped his communicator. "Eno to Central Command, come in."

She held her breath. Could his people actually help them?

"Central Command, come in."

No response.

"Maybe you are too far away, Eno?"

"Yes. That must be it. The last time I communicated was to Transporter Three, but they were in Earth's atmosphere. The Central Command is on the Reliance and she's above Earth's atmosphere, beyond your satellites. I must return to the Concordance and brief the Admiral, my dad. This is something your military must deal with."

"I agree," Bear Hunter said.

"We can't fight the whole town. I'll go with you," Willow Tree said.

Eno took her hand and squeezed it. "As much as I'd love to have your company, Willow Tree, I have no place for you to sleep tonight on the ship. We're pretty full with all the people who are using our Med Beds." He grabbed his boots and put them on.

"I understand." She was disappointed in not being able to go with him, but she didn't want to be compromised either. "I will be going in to work at 3:00 p.m. tomorrow, so let me know what you find out as soon as you can."

He nodded and walked out into the back yard. She followed him out, and walked him to his ship.

She touched his arm. "Please be careful."

"I will. It's you I'm worried about, especially working for someone like the Chief and the mayor." He lifted her chin and kiss her sweetly on the lips.

She put her arm around his neck and kissed him back. Then he pulled her into a tight embrace, returning the kiss with even more passion.

❧ 14 ❧

CONCORDANCE

"We need to get the military involved in this," Eno said.

He paced back and forth in his father's office. The Star Force would be able to help, of course, but they couldn't interfere in another planet's internal problems unless asked. The Earth Alliance was already helping the planet as it was. Too many people working on different projects or missions could actually cause more harm if they weren't all on the same page. His frustration was mounting and he felt powerless in Earth's struggles against this sex trafficking. It was bad enough dealing with the greys, but he never imagined they would stoop this low to cooperate with the raping and killing of children.

"Get me Central Command," Admiral Esrith said into his comm-unit.

"Yes, sir. Go ahead."

"Central Command, this is Admiral Esrith. I just received a report of the reptilians taking human blood and eating their flesh in the New Mexico area on Earth. Can you get this information to General Thompson?"

"Yes, sir. I will have him contact you directly, Central Command out."

"Now, we wait," the Admiral said.

Eno continued to pace. "We can't wait long. We've got to do something to stop this," Eno said. Especially when they were actively raping and killing people this very moment.

The Admiral drummed his fingers on the desk. "How large did you say that tunnel was?"

"I could fly my ship through there."

The Admiral raised his brows.

"I have an idea!" Eno stopped pacing.

"If it's what I'm thinking, you better take someone to help you." He stood and leaned on his desk.

"I've got just the pilots who can help me," Eno said. He rushed out of the office and toward the Lounge. When the door hissed open, there sat his friends. He walked over to the table.

"Who wants to help me kill off a bunch of reptilians and child rapists?"

Torren and Gadara both stood, knocking their seats over.

"We want to help, too," Adam said. Genesis stood beside him.

"When do we start?" Captain Tremol and Keely said, standing.

"Follow me," Eno said. He turned and left the Lounge.

When he reached the flight deck, he stopped and checked with the supervisor. "I need three wing ships, along with Shadow One."

"I need to get clearance first, Lieutenant. One moment."

Eno turned around to see his friends all together. He crossed his arms. "We're waiting for clearance."

Captain Gadara stood beside Torren, her arm over his shoulder. Captain Tremol had his arm around Keely, and

Adam and Genesis had their arms around each other. The only thing missing in this picture was Willow Tree. If only he had her with him now, maybe he wouldn't feel so agitated.

"We can have the ships ready in ten minutes, Lieutenant," the supervisor said.

"Thank you," he said. "We found a tunnel where a ritual was being performed where people were being raped and tortured before the reptilians killed them, drinking their blood and eating them."

"I thought you said there were children involved," Adam said.

"The first one we saw was a small boy. The second one was a young woman, in her teens. Willow Tree's father saw many children in cages."

"Cages?" Genesis asked.

"Yes. This is in New Mexico, where Willow Tree lives," Eno said. "It really bothered me, seeing those images."

"How did you see this without being spotted?" Torren asked.

"Willow Tree, Bear Hunter and I used astral projection."

"You can do that?" Genesis asked.

"Yes. We learned how tonight. Willow Tree's father taught us."

"I got us all wing ships, so we'll be able to fly through the tunnels and take out all those who look reptilian or who are wearing robes," Eno said.

"Just a minute," Admiral Esrith interrupted their conversation. He walked toward the group.

"Yes, Admiral?" Eno asked.

"The U.S. Military will be heading this up. They want to arrest everyone involved, but will fight anyone who resists. They will rescue the children. They have been catching sex traffickers for some time now, so they have a system in place to deal with this sort of thing."

"Is there anything we can do to help, Admiral?" Keely asked.

"You will be their backup and if any grey ships should show up, you know what to do with them, right?"

"Right!" Several people responded in unison.

Eno's spirits were dampened, but he wouldn't give up. He would lead this group and do whatever he had to, to stop this criminal activity.

"Okay, pilots, load up," Eno said.

Once he got clearance to leave the Concordance, he was out, heading to Earth. When he was near the vectors of New Mexico, he contacted Central Command. "Can you patch me through to the military person in charge of this mission on Earth?"

"Certainly. You will be speaking to Captain Moon."

"Captain Moon, this is Lieutenant Eno ni Esrith, of the Concordance, can you read?"

"Eno! It's good to hear your voice. What can I help you with?"

"Actually, I'm calling to offer my assistance to you. I have four wing ships that can fly through those tunnels. We can use cloaking and take out any alien ships down there."

"Great idea! We're almost there. Let me know when you get there."

"Yes, sir." Eno smiled, knowing he was going to be working with Willow Tree's cousin.

He called each ship and told them to use cloaking. When he was within a few hundred feet of the tunnel, he alerted his friends and the captain.

"Did anyone inform you the entrance was a hologram?" Eno asked Captain Moon.

"No. I didn't get that information."

"It's the boulder in front of your tank," he said as he hovered over the tank. The tank moved forward and he followed in behind it.

He alerted each ship of the hologram. "I'll go down the right tunnel, Torren, you take the left tunnel."

"Yes, Lieutenant," Torren said.

"Tremol and Adam, you two stay behind in case any grey ships get past us."

"Yes, Lieutenant Eno," Captain Tremol said.

"Got it!" Adam said.

He flew his ship at a slower speed, watching for movement in the air.

The military men on foot arrested the humans, but shot the reptilians dead.

It appeared they had killed a third person from the two carcasses on the ground beside the altar, and the one half-eaten carcass on top of the altar. How many senseless killings had there been in this little area of New Mexico?

Then, once he was past all the people and chaos, he saw several grey ships with their lights on, in a large opening in the cave. Running toward the ships were several large reptilians. Using his cannon, he blasted two of them when he saw a flash of light coming from his left side, aimed at the other reptilians.

"Boy, that felt good!" Torren called out on his comms.

"Now, let's take out the ships!" Eno said.

"My pleasure," Captain Gadara answered back.

With both ships, blasting away, all four grey ships were down. Eno landed his ship and exited with his new weapon.

"Hey, what are you doing, Eno?" Torren called out on his comms.

"I'm making sure they are dead." He headed for the first

ship, melting it just enough to make sure there were no humans inside. When the grey popped his head out, Eno evaporated him. He got close enough to look inside and found another grey, injured, so he finished him off as well. When he headed to the second ship, he saw Torren and Captain Gadara coming out of the last ship.

"No humans inside, just a couple of dead aliens," Torren said.

"Are you sure they are dead?"

"Absolutely. My Captain here insisted on finishing them off herself. My two shots weren't enough for her." Torren pulled Gadara close and gave her a hug.

"Watch out for their blaster," Eno raised his to show them.

"Where did you get that?" Captain Gadara said.

"From two dead aliens." He pulled the trigger and demonstrated on the last ship and it evaporated.

"Whoa!" Torren said. "I want one of those!"

"You'll have to find one inside one of their ships. I took mine off a hybrid."

"They have hybrids now?" Torren asked.

Eno demonstrated on the third ship, with the button pressed for half power and the entrance melted. All three of them checked the ship and found no one alive, but Eno evaporated the two greys just to make sure.

On the second ship, the ramp came down and two reptilians charged out with the same type of blaster, but Eno was faster on the draw and evaporated both of them, including one of the blasters. The other blaster fell to the ground before the reptilian was evaporated.

"You get your wish, Torren," Captain Gadara said.

As he reached for the blaster, a couple greys popped their

heads out and Eno took one out, but Torren took out the second with his new blaster.

"Well, that was a quick study on new technology," Eno said.

"Yes. I'm a fast learner," Torren said. He raised his new weapon in salute.

"Let's make sure no one else is in this ship," Eno said.

He climbed up into the ship and found a cage with a young woman in her teens. She crouched in the small cage, but she was naked. She looked scared.

"Captain Gadara, we need something to wrap this young woman in. She's still alive, but she needs clothing," Eno said.

Gadara ran back to their ship and grabbed an emergency blanket. After Torren blasted the lock with his stunner, Captain Gadara helped the girl out of her cage and walked her back to their ship.

"We'll take her to the military," Torren said.

"Good, I'll see where this tunnel goes," Eno said.

He climbed aboard his ship and followed down the tunnel a ways until he found a cave-in. Someone had blasted the tunnel from the other side. Well, at least no one else could escape.

He turned his ship around and headed out of the cave, above the military's equipment. He saw Gadara walking the woman to one of the tents the military had set up.

When he checked with his friends, no one had seen any grey ships in the area. The military hauled off all the human criminals and rescued all those in cages. It was a massive undertaking. There were military trucks, buses, and a few tanks surrounding the area. Hovering over the military equipment, he could see tents were set up to give aid to those who needed it.

"Captain Moon, this is Lieutenant Eno again, come in."

"Come in, Eno," Moon said.

"If any of those people need the Med Beds, let us know. We can take a few tonight or send a transporter tomorrow to take groups of them."

"I appreciate that, Lieutenant. I think we'll be okay tonight. We're still assessing the status of the rescued and what is needed. If we think your Med Beds will help, I'll contact the general in the morning," Captain Moon said.

"Hey! There's a ton of alien ships across the sky," Adam called out on his comms.

"Those aren't ours," Captain Tremol said. "I just got intel from Central Command."

"Captain Moon, this is Lieutenant Eno again, come in."

"Go ahead, Eno."

"Do you have any ships in the vicinity?"

"Ships? As in space ships?"

"Yes."

"That would be no, Lieutenant."

"That's all I needed to know, thanks. Eno out."

SKIES OVER NEW MEXICO

The four Concordance ships made their way to the alien crafts without incident. They were all still cloaked.

Eno began the engagement with the greys' ships, but the greys fired back. He blasted the ship from top to bottom, before it wobbled out of the sky, hitting the ground hard.

Torren and Gadara took out another ship, while Adam and Genesis battled with a third. Light flashed between the ships, but only the grey ships could be seen in the skies. For some reason, the greys weren't using their cloaking abilities, but were able to pick up the wing ships even though they *were* cloaked.

Eno took the ship next to Adam and Genesis, taking it down as well. By the time his second ship went down, so did the ship Adam and Genesis had been fighting.

Tremol and Keely took a hit, but not before taking down a greys' ship.

"You two okay there?" Eno asked on his comms. He could see the outline of all four ships on his screen, even though they were still cloaked.

"We're good here," Keely said.

"We show minor damage," Tremol added. "We're heading back to the Concordance while we can."

"Thanks for the help, Captain Tremol. Stay safe."

"Will do."

There were a few more ships to fight and he rejoined the group.

Mescalero Apache Indian Reservation

Willow Tree sat on the back porch watching the skies and wondering what Eno was up to. Touching her lips, she thought of the passion in his kiss and realized he really cared for her. She missed him and he had only been gone a few hours. It was past her bedtime, but after that kiss, she couldn't sleep. Eno had thought about bringing her to the Concordance, but wanted to protect her innocence. What a noble man. She hadn't met any man on Earth who thought that much about a woman's reputation. In fact, they only thought about their urgent needs.

She sat and watched the stars and tried to meditate when she saw several lights moving in the night sky. Those couldn't be stars. She sat up and really concentrated on the lights. It appeared they were getting closer.

She went to her patrol car and popped the trunk. She pulled out the alien weapon, closed the trunk and went back to the porch to watch the skies.

"What is that?" Bear Hunter asked.

"A souvenir," she said. She smiled remembering how she acquired it.

"Is that alien?"

"Of course it is. I took it from the dead aliens that had abducted the two little girls."

"How does it work?" he asked.

"You know those boulders that used to be over there?" She pointed to the open field behind the house.

"Yes. What happened to them?"

She stood and walked to a large rock nearby. She pushed the button before pulling the trigger. Boom! The rock evaporated before her eyes.

"What?" Bear Hunter stood and walked to where the rock had been.

"Cool, huh?"

"The aliens have this technology?"

"The greys do. I don't know about the reptilians." She glanced up and noticed the lights were getting very close.

"Oh my gosh!" She wondered if they were tracking the weapon. "Get inside," she said.

"I will not! This is my home. I stay."

"Fine, Dad." She walked out through the back yard, which was basically a desert. If she could hit one of the ships, it would evaporate it. Were they really that close?

She stood out there, alone, and waited. Finally, the ships moved in. She raised the weapon and aimed at the nearest ship, pulling the trigger. Boom! It was gone.

She raised her other arm in a cheer. "Yes!"

Another one moved in close and she fired again. Boom! Another grey ship down and gone. She repeated her cheer. Then she noticed several more lights coming toward her. The lights were a little different. She watched them. They gained speed on the first couple of lights. Then she saw lights flashing between the different objects.

They were firing on each other! She had no boulders to hide behind, so she moved back toward her home. Finally, one of the objects fell to the ground. She ran toward it to see if it was the grey ship.

It was! She fired on it with the weapon and the ship disappeared.

Another light storm in the sky showed a couple more grey ships. When one got close enough, she blasted it as well. There was at least one more in the sky. She only hoped the Vaedrans were the ones firing against them.

But what fell next from the sky was not a grey ship, but what looked like Eno's ship. She ran toward it. It crashed hard. It suffered a lot of damage from the fight. She pounded on the frame.

"Are you all right in there?"

There was no answer. She pressed the button to lower the power on her weapon and aimed at where the ramp would be. It melted open.

"Eno? Is that you?"

"Willow Tree, wait!" Bear Hunter called out. He was behind her.

"It's not a grey ship, dad."

"Yes, but that one is!" He pointed to the sky.

Sure enough, a grey ship hovered over the Vaedran ship. She flipped the button quickly and hit the grey ship until it evaporated. Then, she climbed up into the Vaedran craft.

Slumped over the Nav-U-Comm was Eno. Oh God, let him be all right! She removed his harness and tried to pull him out. He was heavy. All those muscles add up, she thought. But her military training kicked in. She had to do this in the military, she could do it now. She bent down and draped his body over her shoulder, her weapon in the other hand. She grunted and straightened the best she could and carried him to the door, then jumped down. She could barely stand, he was so heavy. She moved away from the ship, closer to her home. Bear Hunter ran ahead of her and pulled a lounge chair out and helped her lower Eno to the seat.

She checked his pulse. He had one, but was barely breathing. She began her prayer chant to heal him. She gently touched his face and moved her hands down his body, praying over all of him. Bear Hunter stood in prayer as well. She had to block out everything and put all her efforts into her prayer chant.

After a few minutes, she realized someone else stood near her, praying. It was Genesis and Adam. There was no movement from Eno.

Willow Tree stretched across his body, sobbing. Thirty minutes had passed and still he didn't move. She felt a caress on her back.

"It takes time for head injuries," Genesis said.

Willow Tree pulled herself up. "I don't know where he's injured. He was slumped over when I pulled him out."

"She carried him over here by herself," Bear Hunter said.

"From the ship?" Adam asked. He glanced back at the ship and then to the lounge chair.

"Yes," Bear Hunter said.

"Wow, that took a lot of strength," Adam said.

"We can take him to the Concordance to use the Med Beds. Conn can see what is wrong. She, too, is a healer," Genesis said.

"We'll have to carry him to the ship," Adam said.

"We will come too," Bear Hunter said. "Eno has become like family to us."

"We only have room for four. I will alert Captain Gadara. Captain Gadara, come in." Genesis said. She pressed the comms on her wrist.

"This is Gadara. Go ahead, Genesis."

"Eno is injured. We're taking him back to the Concordance but we need your assistance."

"You got it. We've locked on to your location. We'll be there shortly."

"I cloaked Eno's ship until we can bring it back to the Concordance," Adam said.

Yellow Elk had joined them. Willow Tree took Eno's hand and rubbed it. His hands were large and strong. Then she realized his weapon may be in the ship.

"I'll be right back," she said.

She walked to where she thought his ship was. She felt around the outside until she found the opening, and climbed inside. She found his alien weapon and took it with her. She could lock it up in the patrol vehicle with hers. She retrieved her weapon from the back porch, and walked to her vehicle.

"Where did you get a weapon like that?" Adam asked.

"It's a souvenir." She turned and aimed at a large rock and blasted it. It evaporated before them.

"What?" Genesis said.

"Cool," Adam said.

She pressed the button and aimed at another rock and melted it.

"Oh my gosh! The greys are more dangerous than I thought," Genesis said.

"These were taken from hybrids," Willow Tree said.

"Hybrids?" Adam asked.

"Yes, they had sharp teeth. Eno found half-eaten humans inside their ship. The ship that had the little girls I retrieved." She glanced at her father. "Richard was there. He saw it. He's a white hat," Willow Tree said.

"You saw Richard?" Bear Hunter asked.

"Yes."

"I thought he was in Afghanistan?"

"Apparently not. He's working covertly on the sex trafficking sting the President is conducting," Willow Tree said.

"And what is a white hat?" Yellow Elk asked.

"They are the good guys. Right now, Earth is fighting a spiritual battle with good versus evil," Adam said.

Yellow Elk looked at Bear Hunter. "Did you know this?"

"I knew the President was fighting a battle for the children, but I didn't understand the depth of it until we did the astral projections. We saw first hand what evil we are fighting."

Yellow Elk crossed her arms, glaring at Bear Hunter.

"Okay, I will explain it all," he said.

Another ramp opened up nearby and Captain Gadara and Lieutenant Conley came out. Conley ran toward them. He knelt beside Eno, touching his shoulder.

"Hey, big guy. We're here. All your friends are here and we will take care of you."

"How can we assist you?" Captain Gadara asked.

"We need you to take Willow Tree's parents to the Concordance, after you help us get Eno onto our ship," Genesis said.

"How did you get him here?" Lieutenant Conley asked.

"Willow Tree carried him," Bear Hunter said.

Lieutenant Conley glanced at her. "You have my respect, Willow Tree," Conley said.

"Thank you. Part of my military training. You leave no one behind."

Conley, Adam, and Bear Hunter lifted Eno and carried him up the ramp to Adam's ship. They lay him down between the seats. Willow Tree stood outside, waiting.

Conley and Bear Hunter exited and walked toward the cloaked ship with Captain Gadara and Yellow Elk.

"Meet you back on the Concordance," Adam said to the others. Willow Tree and Genesis boarded the ship. She sat next to Eno's head. She fastened her harness and picked up his hand. He looked so helpless and vulnerable. She squeezed his hand and prayed for his healing.

Concordance

Once they were inside the pressurized flight deck, a Med tech came with a hover gurney. Adam, Bear Hunter, and Conley, plus the Med tech, helped get Eno onto the gurney and stabilized him. Soon, they were all headed to the Med Center.

Conn was there and took him immediately. Before she could bring news, Admiral Esrith stood with the small group.

"Who gave him the first treatment?" Esrith asked.

"I'm a healer. I prayed over him but had no results," Willow Tree said.

"It could be a head injury," Genesis added. "They take time to heal. Sleeping like this is normal while the brain repairs itself."

Once Conn came out, she said the same thing Genesis stated.

"Can we see him?" Admiral Esrith asked.

"Yes, but he is still sleeping." Conn showed him the way to Eno's room.

The small group followed him, but waited outside the room.

"Can I stay until he awakens?" Willow Tree asked.

"Of course. There's a chair in the room."

"We will need more chairs," Bear Hunter said. Conn bowed and left the area. It was a long while before Admiral Esrith left the room.

Willow Tree paced back and forth outside the room, while Bear Hunter and Yellow Elk waited in the seats Conn had brought for them. Genesis and Adam, Captain Gadara and

Lieutenant Conley also stood by. Keely and Captain Tremol stopped by and waited also.

When Admiral Esrith emerged from the room, his eyebrows rose. "It makes my heart glad to see Eno has so many friends." He turned toward Willow Tree. "Thank you for helping my son."

"I only wish I could have done more," she said.

He touched her shoulder. "He spoke of you often." Then, he turned to the group. "I want to be informed immediately of any change in status."

"Of course," Conn said.

Willow Tree watched Admiral Esrith walk away. Eno looked so much like him. He spoke of her? Often? She smiled at the thought and walked into the room. She stood on the far side of the bed so she could see the door. She took his hand and kissed the outside of it. Then she caressed his hand.

"You know what works better than kissing his hand, don't you?" Captain Gadara asked.

She glanced up. "No. What?"

Captain Gadara touched her lips with her finger.

"It worked for me," Lieutenant Conley said.

Genesis, Adam, Bear Hunter, Yellow Elk, Keely, and Tremol all squeezed into the small room. "Only five minutes," Conn said, then left the room.

Willow Tree caressed his cheek, then bent down and kissed him tenderly on the mouth. Nothing happened. Disappointment rolled over her. What did she expect? His head injury kept him from responding.

One by one, each person touched his shoulder, said a prayer and then left the room. When it was just Adam and Genesis, Genesis turned to her. "Do you have a communicator?

"Yes," she said. She raised her wrist to show her.

"Call us when he awakens and we will alert everyone else."

"Yes, thank you."

Bear Hunter brought the two extra chairs into the room and he and Yellow Elk held vigil with Willow Tree.

The group that had gathered in the Map Room was large. Admiral Esrith waited his turn in the briefing of what intelligence his team had gathered since the last meeting. In addition to the three admirals and the Joint Chiefs, there were delegates from the Galactic Federation of Worlds, and the Earth Alliance.

"Let's start off with the representatives of the Galactic Federation. Andromedan Councilor Sola?" Admiral Tibbets said.

"Yes. We have much to report," Sola began. "The Moon was important for the greys to control the Earth by sending low frequencies down to Earth through the use of a machine. You will be pleased to know that the Federation, along with the Earth Alliance, have kicked the Orion greys from Nebu, along with the Dark Fleet, off the Moon so that the people of Earth can now control the Moon."

"The Dark Fleet?" Admiral Esrith asked.

"Yes, the Dark Fleet consisted of Germans, descended from the ones the greys worked with in the 1940s, and reptilians, using the ships of the Orion greys," Admiral Johnson of the U.S. Space Force said.

"That accounts for the bases we destroyed from the Concordance?" Esrith asked.

"Correct," Sola said. "In addition, the Dark Fleet based in Antarctica was evacuating and heading for the portal at the South Pole, which was also held by the Dark Fleet."

"It's an inter-dimensional portal," the Pleiadian Councilor, Kalig said. "But the Earth Alliance has taken the portal and dismantled it."

"We were trying to find the frequency key to close all the created portals, along with the natural ones. My sources tell me that the key was found recently," Sola said.

"That's great news!" Admiral Johnson said.

"Yes. Even better, Phobos, a moon of Mars has been liberated as well. It's in the hands of the Federation." Sola said.

"Liberated from what?" Admiral Esrith asked.

"There were captive humans there and they are freed. Phobos is hollow inside, but the Zeta Reticulin, or small greys, treated the abductees to dispatch them as scientific experiments," Sola said.

"I didn't know the extent of the greys in this area," Esrith said. "I am so glad we haven't had to deal with them in anos, in our system."

"Now Deimos is another situation," Sola said. "It's another moon of Mars that has been held by the tall greys. They are exporting humans in slave trafficking."

"Insidious little bastards, aren't they?" Admiral Halsey of the U.S. Navy said.

"You got that right," General Stephens of the U.S. Air Force said.

"The Earth Alliance can use your help in evacuations of these humans from Deimos, Admiral Donner," Kalig said.

"At your service, Kalig," Admiral Donner of the Endeavor said.

"The Interplanetary Corporate Conglomerate has been using captive human slaves on Mars," Sola said. "There are military mercenaries there to protect the ICC facilities against the reptilians and insectoids. The two races are part of the Dark Alliance, working with the Dark Fleet. For years we have been preparing the locals to stand up for themselves and to take back their world. We will need help with evacuations of humans from Mars while we fight the Dark Alliance." Sola glanced around the room.

"If you no longer need the Concordance to patrol the Moon, we will certainly help in those efforts," Esrith said.

"Excellent!" Sola said.

"Are the locals human?" General Thompson of the U.S. Army asked.

"They are worm-like beings who live underground," Kalig said.

"One last thing," Sola said. "The meetings on Jupiter with the Galactic Federation of Worlds and the Earth representatives of Space Programs and corporations are going well. There were about fourteen countries represented the last I heard. My sources will get back to me on that later today."

"What is going on there?" General Thompson of the U.S. Army asked.

"It is a multinational space coalition to determine who will manage the safety zones in this star system. Key to all of this is liberating Mars from the Dark Alliance and freeing the captured slaves. Our Federation is running missions now to make sure no other planet is being controlled by the Dark Alliance," Sola said.

"Yes, and our President is among those attending the Artemis Accords," Admiral Johnson of the U.S. Space Force said.

"Any more news to report?" Admiral Tibbets of the Reliance asked.

"Yes. My pilots have all reported no further incidents with grey ships, except one. He was assigned to the quadrant that is New Mexico of the United States. There was a battle last night and my son was injured. Other pilots are scouring the area for more ships as we speak," Esrith said.

"My prayers for your son, Esrith. My pilots have also reported a decline in grey ships as of yesterday," Admiral Tibbets said.

Esrith nodded to Tibbets as a sign of respect.

"My prayers as well. We also have no new reports since the day before yesterday," Admiral Donner said. Esrith nodded to Admiral Donner as well.

"Our forces are patrolling the skies all over the world with the help of our allies," General Stephens of the U.S. Air Force said. "We've had no other sightings either."

"And our ships are stationed in strategic areas around the world with emphasis on enemy countries who have tried to infiltrate our country both illegally and digitally," Admiral Halsey said.

"I'm afraid we are still fighting the sex trafficking in that same quadrant, Admiral Esrith. We've had reports of another tunnel found. Our military has closed down that tunnel and rescued over forty children and some adults from that location recently. Unfortunately, there has been a rash of illegal entries from the U.S. southern border that affects two different quadrants. We could use some help, on the ground, in rounding up these people. We believe they are dealing in sex trafficking as well. And while our President has been at the Artemis Accords meetings, a clone has taken his place in the White House and is giving contradictory orders, allowing for this illegal entry of persons at the southern border," General Thompson said.

"We will be glad to assist you in any way we can with our technology," Admiral Tibbets said.

"We welcome your help, sir," General Thompson said.

"I have some good news to report," Admiral Johnson said.

"Let's hear it," General Thompson said. "I can use some good news."

"Solar Warden is due in any moment. We will be able to assist wherever we are needed," Admiral Johnson said.

"Solar Warden? What is that?" Admiral Esrith asked.

"It's the Space Force's battleship, you might say. She's been helping the Galactic Federation and Earth Alliance in other parts of the galaxy, battling the Dark Alliance. When she returns, she can help with the Mars situation, or the situation on Earth," Admiral Johnson said.

"What we need is boots on the ground," General Thompson said. "Can anyone help us there?"

"I think I can help you with a small team of eager volunteers," Esrith said.

Concordance

Willow Tree caressed Eno's hand and planted a kiss on his skin when she felt her hand being squeezed. She glanced up and saw Eno smile at her.

"How long have you been here?" he asked.

"All night."

He pulled her closer and hugged her with his other arm. She kissed his warm lips. This time, the kiss was returned.

"I missed you," she said.

"He's awake!" Bear Hunter said. He helped Yellow Elk stand and walk to the bed.

"You two look exhausted," Eno said.

"We are!" Yellow Elk said.

"You try staying awake all night in an uncomfortable chair," Bear Hunter said.

Willow Tree pressed her comms unit. "Willow Tree to Genesis. Eno's awake."

"Got it. We'll pass the word. Genesis out."

"What was that about?" Eno tried to sit up.

Willow Tree propped up his pillows so he could sit up and visit. "Genesis asked me to let her know when you awaken and she would tell everyone."

"Who's everyone?"

"All your friends."

"I don't really have any friends," he said.

"Oh, but you do."

A few pilots came to the room.

"We will be back so you can visit," Willow Tree said. Eno reluctantly let go of her hand. She winked at him and left with her parents.

She passed a few more pilots coming into the Med Center. She found the Cleansing Units the Med tech showed her last night. After relieving herself, she washed up. She must look exhausted, too.

"I'm so glad he's awake," Yellow Elk said.

"Me, too. I don't know what will happen at work today. I'm supposed to fill in for Kyle."

"Your father told me what he saw. Do you think they arrested the Chief and the mayor?"

"I hope so, but I have a suspicion those two escaped," Willow Tree said.

"You can always check with Richard when we get back," Yellow Elk said.

"Yes. I will do that."

She and Yellow Elk joined Bear Hunter outside the cleansing units. The three of them walked back to the Med Center and found a crowd of people inside Eno's room. They waited patiently outside the room while they all visited.

She glanced up and saw Admiral Esrith approach. "Hello Admiral."

He touched her shoulder. "Thank you again for what you did for Eno. Adam told me how you single-handedly carried him out of his wing ship."

"That's the least I could do. I'm afraid I melted your ramp, though."

"How did that happen?"

"I have this alien weapon the greys let me have. I had to open the ramp and that was the only way I could think of to do it."

"We'll send a tech team to Earth to prepare the ship and get it back here for more repairs. Eno's life is more important than any ship," Esrith said.

"You're absolutely right."

Esrith walked to the entrance of the small room. "Can I get a pilot around here?" Esrith said.

A large chorus of "Yes, sir!" sounded and the room cleared out quickly. As the two Esrith men visited, another group of people showed up. Adam and Genesis were joined by Keely and Captain Tremol, Captain Gadara and Conley.

"Looks like the gang is all here," Bear Hunter said.

"Who is with him?" Conley asked.

"His father," Yellow Elk said.

"I guess we wait, then," Conley said.

After a few minutes, Esrith came out of the room. "Oh, just the people I needed to see. Come inside, everyone."

Willow Tree stood with her parents as the others went inside. Esrith stuck his head out the door. "This includes you three." He gestured with his hand for them to come inside.

Esrith gave a short overview of what happened in his earlier meeting with the Galactic Federation and Earth Alliance.

"I can't spare any pilots right now, except this one," Esrith pointed to Eno. "But the U.S. Military needs boots on the ground.

"I can speak to our tribe and see who is available," Bear Hunter said. "The illegals affect everyone in one way or another."

"I'll speak to our community and see if we have anyone who wants to help," Willow Tree said.

"Good." He glanced at his watch. "I expect everyone to be ready to go in about an hour. I'll meet you all on the flight deck." Esrith left the room.

After everyone's visit, Willow Tree helped Eno out of the bed.

"Uh, where are my clothes?"

She realized he had on a very short hospital-type gown.

"Let me ask Conn," she said.

He pulled her arm, "You didn't undress me, did you?"

"No. Not with my parents here, are you kidding?" She touched his chest. "But if I did undress you, you would know it."

He smiled.

In a couple moments, Conn brought his clothes and checked him one more time before releasing him. Willow Tree and her parents waited outside the room for his clearance and then all four of them walked to the flight deck.

"How are you feeling?" she asked.

"Good, but hungry."

"You aren't dizzy?"

"No. Should I be?"

"I'm just making sure, that's all," she said.

He pulled her into a hug and whispered. "Thank you, Willow Tree."

She kissed his cheek, "It was my pleasure."

"Until you finish building your border wall, we can set up a force field that will stop anything from moving through on foot," Captain Tremol said.

"I appreciate that. Then we can concentrate on picking up those who got through and those who have been transported to other states," the Border Patrol agent said.

"How soon can you do this?" Another agent asked.

"We can start now and finish by the end of the day," Captain Tremol said.

"That's a lot of miles," the Border Patrol agent said.

"We got this," Keely said.

He and Keely set up the first of the force field frequency boxes in the California area, while Adam and Genesis did the second set, Captain Gadara and Willow Tree did the third set and Conley and Eno did the fourth set.

"No offense, Captain, but why did they separate me and Eno?"

"Oh, that's because you can't fly and Admiral Esrith doesn't want Eno flying just yet. It wasn't meant to keep you two apart."

"Okay. That makes sense." She felt relieved that it wasn't anything she had done.

The group used two of the cargo transporters for this mission, since the Admiral promised to help the Federation in moving human slaves off Mars. The sooner they got this job done, the sooner they would have two more transporters.

When they finished, Captain Gadara flew them to the next spot along the fence, and activated the previous spot. Every so many miles, they added a double box to strengthen the frequency.

A couple times, they caught up with Tremol and Keely or Eno and Conley. It was her day to work the second shift and when they finally got to New Mexico, she would leave the group. She felt herself dragging as the day grew on. She'd had little to no sleep the night before, holding vigil for a man she was becoming very fond of. In fact, she thought of him often.

In the meantime, Bear Hunter and Yellow Elk rounded up as many tribal people as they could and the Border Patrol deputized them to help in rounding up the illegals.

When Captain Gadara and Conley dropped her off, Eno joined her.

"What are you doing?" she asked. She opened the door to her home. Neither of her parents were there.

"I'm going to help you today."

"There's nothing for you to do, really."

"Oh? What about those people you were going to call who lost their child through abductions?"

She pointed to the sofa. "Wait here, I've got to change," she said. "Oh, and I called all those people. Believe it or not, none of the phone numbers were any good." She walked into her room and stripped off her clothes. She was hot and dusty from the work they had done earlier, so she jumped into the shower. She quickly toweled off and wrapped another towel around her long, wet hair and dressed in a clean uniform. After combing through her tresses, she started braiding it and walked into the living room.

Eno stood. "I wish I could do that." He was very close.

"Do what?"

"Take a shower and change clothes."

She looked him up and down. "You may fit into Bear Hunter's pants, but his shirt may be too short. Use my shower and I'll find something for you to wear." She pointed the way and headed for Bear Hunter's closet.

She found a long dress shirt he never wore and pulled out a pair of jeans from his dresser. She went to place the clothes on the bed and Eno walked out with a towel wrapped around his waist. A very short towel. She couldn't help looking at his well-shaped body.

"Um, sorry. This is all he had. I didn't bring any skivvies."

"What are those?"

"Skivvies? They're underwear."

"Oh, yes. Torren told me about those. We don't wear them."

"Commando. I get it. Well, I'll let you get dressed."

Before she could leave the room, he grabbed her arm and pulled her to him. He wrapped his arms around her, into a hug, and she returned it. But the hug lasted a little longer than what she expected and then it grew into a kiss. Then the kiss grew more passionate and she had to stop it before she did something she wouldn't regret.

"Um, I'm enjoying this."

Eno kissed her neck.

"But I really have to go to work."

He moved the kisses lower and unbuttoned her uniform.

"I'm already in a lot of trouble," she said.

He laughed. "We haven't even started any trouble." He untucked her shirt and kissed her breasts. She pulled him close. She didn't want to stop. But this was her parents' home and she would respect that.

He moved his kisses back to her lips. "We'll continue this later."

"Right." She hurried out of the room and closed the door. That was so close. She quickly re-buttoned her shirt and tucked it back in to her pants.

When he came out dressed, he looked pretty damn hot for an alien. Okay. She had to get her head straight. She was a police officer and she had to act like one.

"I have to get a picture of us." She put her arm around him, raised her arm with her phone and took a selfie of the two of them. She showed him the result.

"I like that. Can I have a copy?" he asked.

"I'll see if I can get one from the drug store." She smiled. He actually wanted a picture of her with him?

"So, let me get something straight, none of the phone numbers were any good?" Eno asked.

She put on her gun belt. "Correct. None of the numbers exist for those people. I copied down all the addresses and today, I plan on visiting all of them to see if I can get any more information."

Eno walked to the patrol car with her. "Did you tell me you had only one detective?"

"Yes. He did all the reports, but the information he took down was minimal."

She and Eno drove to the station. Kyle waited outside in the parking lot for her.

"Hi, Kyle. I bet you're exhausted after working late last

night and early this morning," she said. But not as exhausted as she felt.

"That's not the half of it," he said.

She and Eno got out of the vehicle. "Why aren't you inside where it's cooler?" she asked.

"There's nobody there. The doors were locked this morning. No dispatcher, no Chief. I drove around town and a lot of the businesses never opened today."

"That's odd," she said.

"Do you think your whole town is part of the sex trafficking group?" Eno asked.

"What?" she and Kyle said at the same time.

"Remember last night when we called in the military to arrest those in the tunnels?"

"Yes, but—"

"There were a lot of evil people in those tunnels and a lot of kids in those cages."

"Cages?" Kyle asked.

Willow Tree briefly filled Kyle in on what they had seen when they astral projected into the caverns, following the mayor and the Chief of Police.

"We can probably get a list from Richard on who was arrested," she said. She pulled out her phone and dialed his number, but there was no answer. She texted him to call her.

"Well, I'll keep you posted on what I find out. I guess I can take it from here, Kyle. Did Darryl ever show up today?

"Not that I know of. I did my rounds, checked on the closed businesses, but never heard anyone else on the radio."

A car pulled into the parking lot. It was David Enlow, the night dispatcher.

"Thank goodness David is here," she said. "Eno is riding with me tonight." She touched his arm. Touching him seemed easier to her the longer she was around him.

"Backup! Good deal. Well, I'm off for the next two days. I'll see you in a couple." Kyle left.

"What are you doing outside?" David asked.

"The doors are locked," she said.

"Well, I happen to have a key," David said.

"Great! David, this is Eno ni Esrith and he will be riding with me tonight."

"What are you doing working nights?" David asked.

"It's a long story."

David unlocked the door and they went inside. She filled him in on what had been happening in the past two days.

"Wow. I missed a lot, didn't I?"

"Stay alert, I'll keep checking in with you," she said.

She only hoped she could stay alert with no sleep the night before.

She and Eno left and got into the patrol vehicle. "I guess we'll take a drive downtown and see if we can get anyone to help in this border crisis."

Kyle was right. Hardly anyone was open, except the café.

"Let's start there," she said.

There was a crowd inside the café. She had never seen this many people together at one time in this small town. Not everyone was eating.

"Hello everyone. Kyle tells me that only half of the businesses were opened today. Is something going on I should know about?"

"Who's your friend?" Jeannie, the owner of the cafe, asked.

"This is Eno ni Esrith. He's a pilot from out of town. Are you going to tell me what's going on?" Willow Tree asked.

"That's what we'd like to know," a stranger in the crowd asked.

"Is there some sort of holiday or festival in a nearby town?" she asked.

"Nobody around here closes for that shit," Jeannie said.

"Okay. What do all these closed businesses have in common?"

Silence.

"Was there some sort of meeting last night?" Eno asked.

She had forgotten that the Chief said he would meet the mayor later last night.

"Joe said something about a Freemason's meeting this week," another man said.

"Come to think of it, a lot of those business owners were Freemasons."

"There you go. They must have had some event they were doing somewhere," she said. But were those Freemasons the ones who were arrested? Was that a cult practice to rape and torture children and then eat them?

"Where's Carmela? Where's the Chief?" someone asked.

"Well, has anyone tried calling them or any of the others?" she asked.

"We've been calling them all day and no one answers the phone," Jeannie said.

"Well, I guess we're about to have a town meeting," Willow Tree said. She briefly described what she had seen in her astral body projection and then explained that the military arrested the sex traffickers and rescued the children. She left out the part about the reptilians, but she explained that pilots from the Earth Alliance helped to stop the grey aliens that were abducting people.

"Do any of you know of a family who lost a child to abduction by aliens or just disappeared?" she asked.

Gonzalez was there. "My daughter was taken, but Officer

Moon found her. She was abducted by aliens, as well as Taylor's daughter," he said.

"Illegals?" someone asked.

"No. Aliens from space," Gonzalez said.

Everyone laughed.

"Hey!" Eno shouted them down. "I'm a pilot, like Willow Tree said, but I'm from space. I shot down the ship that had the girls in it. Willow Tree and I rescued the girls after I killed the grey aliens that took them. They had already eaten other people on their ship. Those people that were arrested weren't all humans. Some of them were reptilians from another star system. They have been taking over your planet for thousands of anos. They are shape shifters. They can change into humans and back into reptilians."

"We need your help here," Willow Tree began. "We've got to stop the sex trafficking coming over our borders. We've set up force fields to keep out anything new coming in, but the Border Patrol needs help in rounding up those who are here before they capture anyone else's child."

"Will you help us?" Eno asked.

"You know, there aren't any other children in this area except Gonzalez' kid and the Taylor kid," Jeannie said.

"What happened to all the children?" Willow Tree said.

"I remember a family that lost a child but they moved away," someone said.

"Well, I have a list of addresses here." She pulled out her list from her pocket. "I want you all to look them over and tell me if you recognize any of these addresses, or if you know anything about the families." She put the list on the counter near Jeannie.

Jeannie picked it up and looked it over. "Hell, this one is in my neighborhood," she said. "Nobody lives at this address. The house has been empty for years."

"Do you remember why?" she asked.

"Did a child ever live there?" Eno asked.

"I think there was a child. It was so long ago. I don't remember the details," Jeannie said.

"Anyone here from the newspaper?" Willow Tree asked.

"I think Frank was a Freemason as well," someone said.

"Did he ever print an obituary for anyone?" Willow Tree asked.

"No one reads those," someone said.

"I do," an elderly man said. "I check to make sure it's not a friend of mine. But if someone is missing, they wouldn't be in the obituaries."

"True, but I'm wondering about the families that were left behind. There's no closure for those people. It messes up the family dynamics when someone dies unexpectedly, let alone disappears," Willow Tree said. She remembered some of the families of her fallen brothers and sisters in the military.

"Hey, this is my address," a woman said. "I've been there ten years."

Willow Tree picked up the list and made a note on it so she could check the date later. She also marked Jeannie's neighbor.

"Anyone else want to take a look at this?" She passed the list around and actually got some notes next to the addresses.

"Thanks everyone. Now who is going to help me help the Border Patrol?"

"The sex traffickers aren't just taking children," Eno said. "They've taken teenage girls and boys. Some of those people in the cages were adults," Eno said.

"Adults?" someone asked.

"Yes. We're all neighbors here. We need to watch out for each other," Willow Tree said.

Little by little, people came up to her and volunteered.

She wrote down names and phone numbers. "I'll contact the Border Patrol and we'll get you both together. They need all the help they can get. Now, here's my card." She gave a stack to Jeannie. If anyone remembers any of the families who have lost children or someone to abduction, let me know. We're going to need to know where these recovered children go."

She left the café with Eno and the two of them drove to all the neighborhoods that weren't marked with notes. She had Eno hold her clipboard so they could cross reference the files with the addresses.

By the end of the shift, nothing had panned out. Either the house was vacant, or someone else lived there since the disappearance, but no one remembered the families. How strange.

She and Eno had to drive to the next town to get something to eat since Jeannie had closed her café by dark.

While they waited for their food, Eno took both her hands and began massaging them. "I love everything about you, Willow Tree," he said.

She looked into his eyes. "I feel the same way about you, Eno. I enjoy spending time with you. I'm glad you rode with me tonight. It gets pretty lonely on night shift."

"I thought you only did the day shift."

"When I started out, it was the night shift. Then the Chief was promoted and the day shift was available, so I took it."

When the server brought the food, the conversation ended. It wasn't until they were back in the cruiser before they started talking again.

"Well, at least we have an impressive list of volunteers to help the Border Patrol," she said.

She made her last rounds before heading home around 11:30 p.m. when she got a call on the radio from Ed Davis.

Eno glanced at her. "Who is that?"

"Graveyard shift." She picked up the radio. "Go ahead, 424."

"Where's the dispatcher? And why is the building locked up?"

"Isn't David there? I just talked to him about thirty minutes ago."

There was silence.

"424, come in."

"This is 424. David left a note. He had an early morning appointment and couldn't wait for Carl. He locked up, but Carl has a key. Which does nothing for me," Ed said. "And what are you doing on second shift?"

"A long story. I'm off now, heading home. I guess you're on your own. If you get into trouble, call me."

"Will do, 424 out."

She glanced at Eno and touched his arm. "If it weren't for you, I would have fallen asleep tonight." She yawned. "I'm so exhausted."

"We didn't check with your cousin on the people arrested, did we?"

"No." She picked up her phone and saw the text from Richard. She pulled over to the side of the road to read it. "He says they had over 800 arrests last night and rescued 48 people. Missing two important people, Chief and Mayor."

❧ 18 ☙

MESCALERO APACHE INDIAN RESERVATION

When she parked the patrol vehicle, the back porch light went on. Bear Hunter and Yellow Elk stood on the porch waiting. Both of them had an arm behind their backs.

"What are you two doing up?" she asked. Her parents went to bed early all the time because they awoke early.

Eno was beside her. He grabbed her arm. "Something's not right," he whispered.

She froze in her steps. "I feel it too," she whispered.

"Oh, I forgot something," she said out loud and turned toward the car. She popped the trunk and pulled out the two weapons, handing one to Eno. She swung around and aimed the weapon toward her parents.

Neither of them spoke, but she saw Bear Hunter's arm come out from behind him, and something dark was in it. "You going to tell me what's going on?"

Right before her eyes, they both shifted into reptilians, with guns aimed at them.

She blasted the one on the right and Eno hit the one on the left. The two evaporated.

She ran toward the house. "Oh God, please let my parents be all right."

"Mom! Dad!" she called out as she searched each room.

"Here they are!" Eno called out.

She found him in her parent's closet, untying both her parents.

"Mom!" she hugged her fiercely, then helped her up. Eno had helped her father up and she hugged him, too.

"What happened?" Eno asked.

"The mayor and the Chief of Police came to visit us. They forced us into the closet with their guns. They were waiting on you, Willow Tree," Yellow Elk said.

"How did you stop them?" Bear Hunter asked.

"Eno realized something was wrong and stopped me," she said.

"Yes, but that was brilliant that you said you forgot something," he said.

"What did you forget?" Yellow Elk asked.

"Our alien weapons. I opened the trunk and handed Eno his and I took mine and we shot them both," she said.

"How did you know it wasn't us?" Bear Hunter asked.

"Because you two don't stay up this late and you would have said something to me," she said.

"And you both looked stiff and unfriendly," Eno said.

"Did you evaporate them?" Bear Hunter asked.

"We sure did," she said.

They all went into the kitchen and Yellow Elk poured them all a drink. She handed each of them a glass with some amber liquid.

"What is this?" Eno asked.

"Tequila," Bear Hunter said. "This is a celebration of life. We all survived evil tonight." He raised his glass. She and Eno raised their glasses and so did Yellow Elk.

"We thank the Great Spirit for sparing us this night." Bear Hunter gulped down his drink.

"Amen!" She downed hers, but it burned going down.

"Amen!" Yellow Elk did the same, but she didn't make a face.

"Amen!" Eno made a face, pounded his chest and coughed.

"You all right, Eno?" She patted him hard on the back.

"I've never had anything like it," he said. He coughed again.

She took him by the hand and led him out on the back porch. They sat in the lounge chairs beside each other, gazing at the stars.

"Thanks for saving my life and my parents," she said. She glanced over at him. He glanced at her and took her hand. He pulled it to his lips and kissed her hand. "My pleasure."

"Everything has turned upside down here, Eno. The world is changing and I don't know how to deal with it," she said.

"I think you're doing fine. All you can do is take one day at a time."

They sat there a few minutes holding hands. "I like this," she raised their clasped hands.

"Me. Too."

"What happens now? Will you go back to Vaedra?" she asked. She realized she didn't want to lose him. How could she tell him goodbye?

"After all the greys and the reptilians have been removed from your planet, then, yes, I will eventually return to Vaedra. I will be working with your military white hats to train them to fly our ships."

"That sounds like fun," she said. "You *will* still teach me to fly, right?"

"If you want me to. I'd love to."

"Of course I want you to. I'm off the next two days. I could fly with you and help you with the greys."

"That sounds like a plan," he said.

She yawned. It was so hard for her to stay awake any longer. The tequila helped her relax and she drifted off to sleep. Thoughts of Eno and what could have happened this afternoon if she had let it, played through her mind.

The next morning, she awoke to birds chirping and the sun shining. She stretched and realized she had slept on the lounge chair all night, but she had a blanket covering her. When she glanced around, there was Eno, in the lounge chair next to her. He also had a blanket, but he was propped up watching her.

"How did I—?"

"I covered you up and got a blanket for me as well. Your mother had two blankets sitting on the dining room table."

She reached over and took his hand. "I like waking up beside you in the morning."

"We can make it permanent if you like?"

She sat up. "What?"

"If you will be my mate, we can make it permanent."

"I think I'd like that very much."

"It's settled, then." He sat up and pulled her into a standing position. Then he pulled her close, kissing her passionately. She returned the kiss, savoring every minute of it, her arms wrapped around his neck and shoulders.

"Breakfast is ready," Yellow Elk called out.

"Perfect timing," he said.

Both her parents were at the table when she and Eno walked in. He held her hand.

"Good morning!" Eno said to both of them.

"You look happy today," Bear Hunter said.

"I am happy. I would love your blessing for me and Willow Tree. She consented to be my mate," he said.

Yellow Elk stood and hugged Willow Tree. "I am so happy for you, my Willow Tree." Then she hugged Eno. "I am happy to welcome you into our family."

Bear Hunter stood and hugged Willow Tree and then Eno. "You are already part of our family. You have my blessing. Both of you," he said.

"We must plan the ceremony," Eno said. "We do things one way in our culture on Chroma, but I would like to do the ceremony as your people do it on Earth," Eno said.

Willow Tree reached up and kissed his cheek. "Thank you, Eno," she said.

"You will be Willow Tree Eno after the ceremony," Eno said.

"It isn't Esrith?"

"That is my father's name. My name translates as Eno, son of Esrith. You will be known as Willow Tree, mate of Eno."

"Well, that's different."

Eno raised his eyebrows.

"But I'm okay with it," she said. She kissed him again on the cheek and they all sat down to eat breakfast.

Reliance

Admiral Tibbets glanced around the Map Room. "We will begin our update with Andromedan Councilor Sola."

Sola stood up. "The Earth Alliance is helping Solar Warden in clearing out the Dark Fleet on Ceres and returning the planet to the humans who have been liberated. We've left a contingency of forces there to help them start the process of forming their own government and will leave as soon as they've set something up."

"Thank you, Sola. Now let's hear from Pleiadian Councilor Kalig," Admiral Tibbets said.

Kalig stood to address everyone.

"Thank you, Admiral. The Galactic Federation of Worlds has ships out over Phobos and Deimos, making sure the Dark Fleet does not return. The Endeavor is about finished evacuating the humans from Deimos. On Mars, we have finally returned the planet to the indigenous creatures who inhabit it. Thanks to the pilots of the Concordance, we have most of the humans off Mars. The Dark Fleet and their allies are gone. We have a group working with the Martians to help them establish some form of government since they have been battling for the planet for years," he said.

Esrith raised his hand.

"Yes, Admiral Esrith?"

"We just completed a mission on Earth to help close off a section of wall from illegal entry of foreigners to United States soil. I still have a small group of volunteers out helping to eliminate the greys' ships over the planet. They should be on their way by the end of the day, Earth time," he said. He hoped that was true. He had to round up everyone before leaving the moon's upper atmosphere. After the ceremony honoring their fallen heroes yesterday, everything fell behind.

"I do have a question for the Federation, though," Esrith began.

"Go ahead," Admiral Tibbets said.

"After our pilots leave Earth, who will take up the fight for the greys' ships trying to escape Earth?" Esrith asked.

"We will," Tibbets said. "We are spread thin right now,

but we do have pilots all around Earth, taking out the ships trying to leave."

"And we will get those who happen to get through," Kalig said.

"The U.S. Military and their allies should be wrapping up the sex trafficking soon. We are about finished. We found an unexpected, deep tunnel in New Mexico the other day and were able to rescue quite a few people but we arrested practically a whole town," General Thompson of the U.S. Army said.

"Very good," Admiral Tibbets said.

"We should be able to disclose the truth to the people within a week or so," Admiral Johnson of the U.S. Space Force said.

"Very good. Does that mean we will be finished with this mission?" Admiral Donner asked.

"Absolutely," Kalig said. "However, we will keep a fleet over Earth's Atmosphere to monitor the planet for a while longer to make sure no other Dark Fleet or Forces return."

Concordance

Esrith arrived on his ship and spoke to the Ensign on communications. "Yes, I want all the pilots recalled to the ship as well as our volunteer crews. They must be back by mid-day."

"Yes, sir."

"Also, let me know the progress of Shadow One's repairs."

Esrith headed to his office to tackle some unresolved paperwork. All the ships must be serviced before arriving in Mars' atmosphere. The few pilots he had already sent had ships that were overdue for servicing. Hopefully, there would be no more problems.

Mescalero Apache Indian Reservation

Willow Tree and Eno headed into town in her convertible Volkswagen Bug. She had the top down and enjoyed the New Mexico sunshine and the handsome man sitting next to her.

"So, you always cook on your days off?" Eno asked.

"Yes. My mother cooks all the other times. Besides, one day, I'll be cooking for you, so you will get to taste my cooking tonight."

Eno played with her hair while it blew in the wind. "I like your hair like this," he said.

"I should have pulled it back. It will be all tangled when we stop."

He leaned over and kissed her cheek. Today was theirs. She felt Eno belonged to her and nothing else mattered.

"Did you hear from your friends about your ship?" she asked.

"Captain Tremol said he would let me know when she's fixed," he said.

"She?"

"We always refer to ships as feminine."

"Yeah, I guess our military does too."

"Willow Tree this is Genesis, come in."

She glanced at Eno. She pressed her comms on her wrist. "This is Willow Tree, go ahead."

"We've been trying to reach Eno but he's not responding. Is everything all right?"

Eno reached for his shoulder, but forgot he wore Bear Hunter's shirt and didn't have his communicator on.

"Yes, everything is fine. He forgot to wear his comms unit and he's with me," she said.

"The admiral is calling everyone in. We need to be back by mid-day. We have a new assignment on Mars. He is the last to be notified."

"He has no ship. How can he return?" she asked.

"We can pick him up. What's your location?"

"We're on Hwy 54, heading into town, but I can head back home if that will work for you?"

"Yes, we've got that location in our database."

"We're on our way back," Willow Tree said.

Eno touched her shoulder. "I was looking forward to spending the day with you." He sounded disappointed.

"Yeah, me too." She slowed the car down and turned sharply left and headed back home.

"Do you know how long you will be gone?" she asked.

"No. I'm not even sure what this mission is about."

"Well, if you're leaving then that means the white hats must have won," she said. She tried to be optimistic.

"I will be back and we will live on one of the bases where I will be teaching flight skills."

"And after that?"

"After that I will still have my time in the Star Force and you can either live here on Earth or on Chroma until I'm finished."

"Are you saying I will be living without you for the next six years?"

MESCALERO APACHE INDIAN RESERVATION

Willow Tree stood on the back porch, holding onto Eno. His arm was around her.

She took a deep breath. If she spoke, she felt she would cry. She glanced up at him and his jaw was clenched. She was already missing him. Rising on her toes, she kissed his cheek. He turned and kissed her lips, hugging her tightly.

She hugged him back and the kiss grew more passionate and she didn't want it to stop.

"Eno!" Adam called out.

Damn. She leaned her forehead against his. *'I love you Eno ni Esrith with all my heart,'* she projected with her mind.

'I love you, too, Willow Tree Moon, now and forever.'

They pulled apart. "Did you just speak to me telepathically?" she asked him.

"Yes, I did and I heard you telepathically. I will send you thoughts until I'm back."

She handed him his comm-link and his alien blaster.

He lifted her chin and kissed her once more on the lips, then left.

She watched him walk off in his pilot's unicrin, he called it. Her mother had washed it for him last night. When the ship rose in the air, it disappeared, and the tears streamed down her face.

She felt an arm around her. She glanced sideways and saw her mother.

"I will miss that boy," Yellow Elk said.

Bear Hunter joined them on the porch. "I believe he will be back," he said.

Willow Tree glanced at her father.

"Yes, Eno is a man of his word." Bear Hunter turned and went inside.

Transporter One

Eno sat several seats back in the transporter, mentally making plans for his future. After they were in space, Adam came back to talk to him.

"You okay Eno?"

"Why wouldn't I be?"

"You look sad."

"No sadder than you if you couldn't see Genesis for an unspecified amount of time."

"I get your point. I don't think I could handle it. No, in fact, I know I can't. I tried that early on when she took me back to Earth from the Vaedra system. I was sick, just thinking about leaving her."

"You are absolutely no help at all."

Adam shook his head and went back to the Nav-U-Comm.

Concordance

Inside the Map room, Admiral Esrith gave the pilots instructions on the rescue of the human slaves from Mars. The pilots were to go in and shoot any reptilians or insectoids, making way for the transporters to come in and get the people out.

"The intel we have is that the Dark Forces are gone, but if you see any of those creatures, shoot to kill. The natives of Mars are worm-like creatures and they are not to be harmed," the Admiral said.

"Are we bringing the people back to the Concordance?" Captain Tremol asked.

"Yes. They will go through the Med Beds, checking for injury or implants," the Admiral said.

"Where will they go from there?" Keely asked.

"Once we've established they are fit to travel, we will be transporting them to a Federation ship where all the displaced people will either be returned to their homes, or they can choose a new life on a planet or moon in the Saturn system."

"Saturn system?" Adam asked.

"Yes. There's a colony of humans there who had been abducted by other greys. They chose to live there rather than go home for whatever personal reasons they had. There's a military base there to protect them from other ETs who may show up and we have a Federation ship that will patrol the space in that system until the Artemis Accords go into effect," the Admiral explained.

"Okay, what are the Artemis Accords?" Conley asked.

"It's a treaty of sorts, set up between several countries and corporations to establish peace in the galaxy and also determine who will lead these nations in the exploration of space."

Conley glanced at Captain Gadara. "We will get to set up a base somewhere after all, baby."

"How long do you think this mission will take?" he asked his father.

"We will be there until all the humans are rescued and all the Dark Fleet and Orion greys are gone. Some of you have already been helping in this matter, but all the ships need servicing, that's why I called everyone in. We don't need any mishaps."

"Is there anyone staying on Earth to take out the greys and reptilians?" one of the pilots asked.

"Yes, the Reliance's pilots will deal with the Dark Fleet on Earth," the Admiral said.

Mercy, New Mexico

Willow Tree went into town with her mother. She would still have to prepare dinner for the three of them. As she drove through town, she noticed a lot of businesses were still closed.

"What's happened?" Yellow Elk asked her.

"All those people who were arrested came from this town. Pedophilia and murder are strong cases. I hope those that were involved in that horrible satanic ritual never see the light of day."

"I didn't realize how much that affects this town," Yellow Elk said.

"I know. And this is only one town. The white hats have been after the sex traffickers all over the world. The *whole world*. This sin is so deep, it's affecting everyone. And all those children. How will we find their parents? I've looked for the families of the missing children in this town and they are all gone."

"How many families?" Yellow Elk asked.

"Twenty-five families have disappeared. Did you read

about it in the papers? Was it on the local news?" Willow Tree asked.

"I don't remember seeing anything about them," Yellow Elk said.

Willow Tree pulled along the curb and parked her car. "Looks like the grocery store is still open," she said.

"Willow Tree, look! The dress shop is open. Let's go in there first."

"Why?"

"You are going to be Eno's mate. We have to find something for you to wear besides jeans and t-shirts," Yellow Elk said.

She took a deep breath. Looking for a ceremonial dress would make her feel better.

Willow Tree and her mother went inside the shop and looked around. The shopkeeper moved her newspaper enough to acknowledge their presence.

"Here are some white dresses," Yellow Elk said.

Willow Tree glanced at them. "They're all sundresses."

"That would be perfect for you now. It's still warm and you look good in white with your coloring."

She gave them a second look and took a couple in the dressing room to try on. One looked better than the other and showed off her figure. Wearing a uniform and gun belt every day did nothing for how she really looked. She changed back into her jeans and t-shirt and brought out her pick.

The shopkeeper was standing next to her mother.

"I like this one," she said.

"You *are* the one," the shopkeeper said.

"The one what?" Willow Tree asked.

"The one the article is about." The shopkeeper went to her register and pulled out the newspaper. On the front page was a headline, "UFO IN MERCY, ABDUCTS TWO CHILDREN."

She continued reading. It was her report, but the author of the article made it look more impressive. "Too bad there wasn't a photo," she said. She really meant it. And she could've taken a picture, she just never thought about it.

"Oh, yes, that would have been awesome."

Then she remembered Eno wanted a photo of the two of them.

"How much do I owe you?" Willow Tree asked.

The shopkeeper rang up the sale. "$53.70."

Willow Tree pulled out her wallet and handed the clerk her card. "Is the drug store open?"

"Yes, I think it is. And so is the café, but I think that's it."

The shopkeeper handed Willow Tree the package and her card.

"Thank you," she said.

"Will we still have police protection in this town?" the shopkeeper asked.

"There are only a few of us left. Didn't anyone patrol today?"

"No. We haven't seen anyone patrolling since your last shift."

Willow Tree and Yellow Elk left the dress shop. "Darryl was supposed to pick up the slack on my off days," she said.

"Well, maybe he's at the office," Yellow Elk said.

"Hmm, I might check that out later. In the meantime, I need to print a photo for Eno and for me," she said.

They walked across the street to the drug store. The clerk helped her retrieve the photo and submit it for printing.

"Make four copies," Yellow Elk said.

"Four?" Willow Tree asked.

"Yes, one for each of us." Yellow Elk smiled.

They waited for the images to print and wandered around the store. Willow Tree found a couple of small frames and paid for them. When the images were finished, she put one in each of two frames.

"That's a nice touch," Yellow Elk said.

"What are you going to do with yours?"

"Mine will go in my album," she said. She opened her purse and pulled out a 4x6 album and put the image into it, next to a younger image of Willow Tree in her military uniform.

"The other one will be for Bear Hunter," she said.

The two of them shopped for groceries for the week and headed home.

"I should stop by the station and see if anyone is there," Willow Tree said.

"No, we have too many groceries. We need to go home," Yellow Elk said.

"You're right. I just feel responsible for the lack of police protection. I should be working instead of enjoying my day off."

"Nonsense. You aren't the Chief and you aren't responsible for this debacle. The whole town needs to decide what will happen next."

"That's brilliant, Mom! We need a town meeting."

"Not today. Wait until you go back to work. Tomorrow, we plan your ceremony."

Mars

One after another, the pilots of the Concordance flew into the interior of Mars. The tunnels were huge, much like those on Earth. They rarely had to use their cannons. They only encountered the reptilians or insectoids when evacuating the humans, since they were still being guarded by these creatures. To allow for maximum evacuation, the pilots stood guard while the crew of the transporters herded the humans to safety.

The first run went smoothly, and the first transporter returned to the Concordance. There were four escorts for each transporter.

"Second run, everyone ready?" Eno said to his team of pilots.

"That's a go, Shadow One," the next pilot announced.

Into the interior, Eno shined his ship's light, with nothing showing but the bare walls of the tunnel. Once they arrived at the compound, a few reptilians shot at them from outside the doors. Eno fired his cannon, hitting one of the reptilians.

"Got one!" another pilot said, as the second reptile went down.

"Stay alert," Eno said. He landed his ship and took his new weapon with him. When they entered, an insectoid-like creature jumped out at them, but he finished him off quickly.

Adam and Genesis herded the next group of humans into the transporter, while two other pilots stood guard outside the ship. All the tunnels had air running through them, but the exterior of the planet was not habitable due to lack of oxygen.

Before the last of this group got into the transporter, he took a look around the compound. He saw movement off to his left and swung around, blasting the reptilian hiding in the shadows.

"This compound goes on forever," he said into his comms.

"We're full and ready to head out," Adam said.

"On my way," Eno said. He visually scanned the area as he headed back to the ship.

Another group went out with Transporter Three and again with Transporter Four.

By his second time through, the number of reptilians and insectoids dwindled. They still had to go in on foot, searching for the captives. The trip was deeper into the compound, taking longer. By the time they reached the captives, the group was small and there were no reptilians left, only a few insectoids. He finished them off quickly and loaded up the captives.

"Anyone else in this place?" Eno asked.

"No, we are the last," the captive said.

"Are you sure?" Eno asked.

"Yes, yes. I'm sure. I've been all over this place, working. We can check as we go out," the captive said.

So they did, one room at a time.

"I think we've got them all," one pilot said.

"Don't be so sure. Stay alert," Eno said. He had a feeling it wasn't over. Not yet. "I'm not seeing anything, but stay alert." He turned all his sensors on his scanner to pick up any movement. He could see Adam and Genesis from the transporter searching the cavernous hall, looking for openings, along with the three other pilots.

"I think I found something," Adam said. Using a plasma bomb, he popped the door open. Two insectoids came running out, but Eno hit them with his new blaster, evaporating them.

"All clear," Adam said.

After a few minutes, Genesis and another pilot led a small group of people into the transporter. Two pilots followed them out and they took off.

Eno and another pilot followed the transporter, escorting it to the Concordance. Once everyone was safely unloaded onto the larger ship, the team was to return to Mars.

This was just the first tunnel. There were several more around Mars that held captives.

Each team was successful, but the mission took another two days to accomplish with little sleep and four-hour rotations.

By the time he returned to the Concordance for the last time, he was exhausted. But before he closed his eyes, he sent a thought to Willow Tree, as he did each time he returned.

'I love you Willow Tree Moon, now and forever.'

And Willow Tree would respond, *'I love you Eno ni Esrith with all my heart.'*

He waited for her response, like always, but this time, it didn't come.

❧ 20 ☙

MERCY, NEW MEXICO

Willow Tree had called all the police officers of Mercy and told them about the town meeting. All except Darryl Kline. He didn't answer his phone, so she left a text message. For all she knew, he was arrested with the Chief. And Carmela didn't answer, either. She made a few flyers and put them up around town, while she and her mother went to the next town to do some shopping.

"So, you're going to have the town meeting at 11 a.m. at the café, but you're meeting with the police officers at 10 a.m.?" Yellow Elk asked.

"Yes. We have to have some sort of strategy. We don't have enough officers to cover all the shifts anymore."

"Maybe we can get some people to volunteer for dispatching and have the trained dispatchers pick up the shifts," Yellow Elk said.

"That's a wonderful idea. I'll bring that up at the meeting."

They headed for Three Rivers to see if they could find some blankets to use for the ceremony. She didn't know when

Eno would return but she wanted to put together a ceremony that would mean something to both of them.

"Since all the family lives on the reservation, Bear Hunter and I can hand-deliver the invitations for you," Yellow Elk said.

"Oh, no. I forgot to write them. I'll have to do that when we get home." She had too many things to think about. The town was falling apart, the love of her life was gone, a wedding to plan, invitations to write. "Does it ever get any easier?"

"Planning a wedding is the hardest thing I had ever done. My advice is keep it simple," Yellow Elk said.

"Thanks, Mom." She squeezed her mother's hand.

Later that evening, before she went to bed, she heard Eno in her head. *'I love you Willow Tree Moon, now and forever.'*

She returned, *'I love you Eno ni Esrith, with all my heart.'*

The next morning, Willow Tree patrolled the town, making sure everything was as it should be. The few businesses that opened early were opening as she drove through town. It would be 10 a.m. before she could get into the station, so she drove down highway 54 and into the subdivisions, down country roads. She took her time and everything seemed peaceful.

She felt a little anxious, taking on this responsibility, but someone had to do it. None of the other officers stepped up to address the situation.

She pulled into the parking lot and waited for everyone to show up. One by one, the officers arrived, all of them dressed in their uniforms.

David came and unlocked the door. They all crowded into the station, sitting on the desks, rather than in the seats.

"So what did you have in mind, Willow Tree?" Kyle asked.

"First of all, there are three people missing. I haven't heard from Carmela or Darryl. Have any of you been able to reach them?" she asked.

They all shook their heads.

"What about the Chief?" Sid asked.

She explained what happened on the night of the out of body experience and how over 800 people were arrested.

"Eight hundred people?" Ed Davis asked.

"Yes and they are all from this town. Because the charges are murder and crimes against humanity and pedophilia, none of them will be coming back."

"They always get away with murder. They will be back," Sid said.

"They were sent to Gitmo and for their crimes, it's the death penalty," she said.

"How do you know this?" Carl Taylor asked.

"She has inside information," Kyle said.

"Yes, but it's limited. What we need to decide is who is willing to run the Police Department from here on out and who will pick up shifts until we can hire others to fill Carmela and Darryl's positions and we need another swing shift person," Willow Tree said.

Everyone looked at each other.

"I have a suggestion. Actually, my mother suggested this, but if some of you who are dispatchers are willing to do a shift, maybe we can get volunteers to train to do dispatching until we can hire someone. What do you think?"

"That's an excellent idea," Carl said. "I'd be willing to pick up a shift."

"Me, too," David said.

"Great," Willow Tree said. "That's a start. Here's a weekly calendar. Fill in the shifts you're willing to take and we'll go from there."

"So what are you planning for the town meeting?" Kyle asked.

"I was planning on telling them the truth and let them decide what to do about our little town. Do we even need a mayor? And what are we going to do about those businesses that are closed?" Willow Tree asked.

"How are we going to get paid without the mayor?" Sid asked.

"That's a good question. Hopefully, someone at the meeting might have an answer to that," she said.

"While we are at that meeting, I suggest we make keys for all of us. This is ridiculous that there's only one key," David said.

"Since you have the only key, I suggest you take care of that problem for now, David," she said. "Now who has the key to the Chief's office?"

David walked over to the Chief's door and tried the key. The door opened.

"Well, there you go," Kyle said.

Willow Tree took the calendar that was filled out and made a copy for each of them.

"Okay, this is our schedule for now. If anyone needs time off, we'll have to double up on shifts or hire a temporary person to fill in," she said.

"If we can find volunteers today, when do you want us to start training the dispatchers?" Carl asked.

"Right away," she said. "We still need some police officers, so we'll see what happens today."

They all headed to the café in their own vehicles.

Everyone was there, so Willow Tree explained what had happened a few nights ago. She laid it all out and people started talking and offering suggestions.

"Is there anyone here from the mayor's office?" she asked.

A woman raised her hand. "I was a secretary before Mayor Rey came to power. I can remember a lot of what we did there. I'll be glad to fill you in later," she said.

Willow Tree took her name and phone number.

"Since the mayor is an elected official and he is deceased, I say we call for a vote," Ed Davis suggested.

"Yes," several people said at once.

"I think we need someone to nominate someone else," Bear Hunter said.

"I nominate Jeannie," a voice called out.

"Who, me?" Jeannie asked.

"Yeah, I second that," someone else said.

By noon, they had a new mayor and Willow Tree was the new Chief of Police, with Carl as the assistant Chief.

"Well, this has been the best turnout for voting in Mercy history," she said.

"Yes, 100% turnout," Yellow Elk said.

The call for volunteers turned up three new people for dispatching, including her mother.

"The Police Department is now hiring," Willow Tree said.

The town's people decided to sell the closed businesses and pay off the mortgages that were on them and keep the rest for operating expenses for the town, like the Police Department and the Volunteer Fire Department. The rest, they would figure out as they went along.

Willow Tree continued doing her regular shift without a

dispatcher for a while, while the volunteers were being trained.

It worked out that everyone stayed on a straight shift, they either dispatched a few days or patrolled a few days, so all the new people were scheduled accordingly.

By the end of her shift, she was ready to go home. It seemed like a very long day and she was beat. After changing clothes, she sat out on the back porch and drank a cold beer.

"One of those days, huh?" Yellow Elk said.

"Well, today definitely was," she said.

"Now that you're the new Chief of Police, what will you do to make this town safer?" Yellow Elk asked.

"Well, I've always thought the town was safe. But no one knew about the evil going on under the surface. I'll just keep vigilant and patrol like I usually do, instead of sitting in an office all day. Plus, all the officers will get more training on detective work, making us all detectives."

"I start my training this afternoon," Yellow Elk said.

"Good for you."

"Yes, I'll be working your shift. I will be your new dispatcher."

Willow Tree smiled at the thought, then heard Eno in her head. *'I love you Willow Tree Moon, now and forever.'* She missed him dearly. She pictured him in her mind, his pale blue eyes, his white-blond hair. *'I love you Eno ni Esrith, with all my heart.'*

The next morning, Willow Tree and her mother drove to the station, early in the morning. She showed her mother where everything was.

"There's usually not much going on. As long as you can call for backup of the nearest town's Police Departments or our fellow officers, or the volunteer firefighters, that's the main thing." She handed her the list of those numbers. "You can read or knit, or whatever, as long as you can answer the radio and the phone."

"You know I don't knit. I am a weaver," Yellow Elk said.

"Yes, and you do beautiful work." She kissed her mother's head. "I promise I'll call in more than I did in the past, but you wouldn't know about that."

"10-4," her mother said. "I have the code book to read for today."

"Very good." She poured herself a cup of coffee and one for her mother. "I'll see you around lunchtime if not sooner."

By the time she got settled in her patrol vehicle, she called in for her mother's practice.

"421 is 10-8," she said.

"10-4."

She smiled as she drove down the road.

Today, she stopped at every opened business and made sure they felt comfortable in calling the police if anything felt out of place or anyone looked suspicious.

"You know you're somewhat of a celebrity around here, don't you?" Jeannie asked her.

"A celebrity?" she laughed. "Why?"

"That UFO article. Everyone is talking about it."

"Well, hopefully we won't have any more of those around here. And I hope we won't see any more reptilians, either."

"I had to call Three Rivers to get some 'For Sale' signs.

But I will be posting them all over town on the closed businesses," Jeannie said.

"Good. If you need any help, let me know."

"No, I'm putting my retired husband to work. He will be managing this café when I have to do the mayor stuff. I think he was getting bored at home anyway, so this is perfect. Besides, we have a lot of people out of work because of the closed businesses. I think you'll find a few good police officers real soon."

Willow Tree continued her patrols, going down every road and subdivision in the town. All was quiet. By the time she finished her rounds, it was close to lunchtime. She had called in every time she left her vehicle, just to keep her mother on her toes. She never did that with Carmela. She would make a point to get the other officers to do the same. They had all gotten sloppy over time. It was all about training. She made a note to put it in a memo. That was easier than calling a meeting. As she pulled into the parking lot at the station, she called in on the radio.

"421 will be 10-7 for lunch."

There was no response. "Hmmm." Maybe she was in the bathroom. She waited a few minutes and then tried again.

"Dispatch, come in. This is 421, do you read?"

No response. She grabbed her clipboard and her portable radio and exited the car. Hopefully, her mother was just in the bathroom.

The door to the station was unlocked. Did she lock it when she left? She couldn't remember, but it had never been locked before. Maybe she was just paranoid after all the things that had happened recently.

"Mom?" she glanced around the office. The four officer's desks were sitting neatly empty. She glanced at the corner desk where the dispatcher was supposed to be, and her mother wasn't there.

She headed to the back room where there were two bathrooms, one for men and one for women and the break room area. The table with four chairs was empty.

She went back to the bathrooms. The women's door was locked.

"Mom? Are you in there?"

There was no answer. She knocked on the men's room and tried the door. It was unlocked and empty.

She went back to the women's bathroom, her adrenaline pumping. She pulled out her keys and tried them on the bathroom. None of them worked. She ran to the Chief's office. It was her office now. Searching through drawers, she found a set of keys. She fumbled through them, trying all of them on the door until it finally unlocked.

Inside, on the floor, was her mother, bound and gagged.

Before she could untie her mother, something hard came down on her head.

MERCY POLICE STATION

Willow Tree woke up dazed. She was in a dark place. Something was over her mouth and in her mouth. It felt like cloth. She blinked her eyes, trying to adjust to the darkness.

Her hands were bound behind her and her feet were bound as well. She tried to straighten her legs, but something blocked them. She sensed something else near her, but she couldn't tell what it was.

It was so dark, she couldn't see anything, even after her eyes were accustomed to the darkness. Where was she? What time was it? Surely she would be missed. And her mother? She didn't even know if she was alive. But why would someone tie her mother up, if she weren't alive? That didn't make any sense.

She sniffed the air. A little metallic, maybe? Where she lay was flat and padded, somewhat. She wiggled around. A blanket maybe?

She summoned all her military and police training. She would not panic. She had to think straight, but her head hurt.

She remembered getting hit hard on the back of the head. Did her mother suffer the same way?

Something moved beside her. It hit her foot. But she couldn't talk. "Mmmm!"

"Mmmm, mmmm."

She projected a thought. *'Mom? Is that you?'*

"Mmmm!" *'Yes, Willow Tree, it's me.'*

Oh, God, please let her be all right. She concentrated again. *'I'll try to get help.'* She projected her thoughts to her father. She knew he could hear her. *'Dad, it's me, Willow Tree. Mom and I are bound and gagged. We were at the Police Station. Help us.'*

Sid Reed glanced over the log book.

"Hmm. There's nothing after 11:30 am. That's odd. I want you to log everything," Sid said.

"You mean every time you say something and the time?" Daniel asked.

"Yes, exactly, like Yellow Elk did." He glanced around the office. "It's not like Willow Tree to not sign out for the day or brief the next shift on what's happened."

"Isn't that her patrol car out there?" Daniel asked.

"Yes. Which means, she's either still here or she got a ride home some other way."

"That doesn't make sense if you all have a vehicle to drive home."

"You're absolutely right," Sid said. "I'm going to look around. I've got my portable, so stay close to your radio." He unholstered his weapon. Something definitely didn't feel right.

He checked both bathrooms and the break room. Nothing.

He went into the Chief's office. Nothing there. Nothing in the file room. "I'm going to check around outside."

Sid walked slowly around the building, but saw nothing. The Police Station sat at the end of town, so there was nothing close by to hide in.

"Dispatch, this is 422, I'm going on patrol," Sid said.

"10-4," Daniel responded.

"Call me on the radio or my cell if you hear from 421."

"10-4."

Sid drove through town but didn't see anything unusual. He decided to stop by the café, since Jeannie seemed to know everything that went on in town.

"Yeah, she stopped by this morning, but she didn't come by this afternoon. She usually makes her rounds twice a day."

Sid left, still puzzled as to what had happened. He continued his rounds through town and the highway and all the side roads. By the time he made all the routes, he headed back to the station to check on Daniel. When he pulled into the parking lot, an old red pickup sat next to Willow Tree's vehicle.

"422 to dispatch, come in?" He called from his vehicle.

"This is dispatch, go ahead 422."

"There's a suspicious looking truck in our parking lot. Have you seen anyone around today?"

"10-4, that would be Willow Tree's father. He's here to see you."

"10-4." Sid exited his vehicle. Maybe Bear Hunter knew something.

"Bear Hunter, how are you?" Sid asked.

"I got a message from Willow Tree a little while ago. I got here as fast as I could."

"You talked to her?"

"No. We're telepathic. She said she and her mother were bound and gagged. They were at the police station."

"I checked everywhere and there is no sign of either of them." Sid picked up the log book. "Look, there are no entries past 11:30 am."

"She's been missing that long?"

"We don't know. She wasn't here at 3 p.m. when we got here."

"She contacted me around 4 p.m."

Sid glanced at his watch. It was 5:30 p.m.

"See if you can contact her again," Sid said.

"I've tried, but there was no response. I tried contacting her mother, and she didn't respond either."

Concordance, over Mars

"Something's happened to Willow Tree," Eno said. He paced back and forth in his room, his empty cup on the table next to Torren.

"How do you know?" Torren asked. He sat in Eno's only chair, enjoying a drink over their successful mission.

"Before I left, I learned she was telepathic. We've been speaking to each other each night but tonight, she didn't answer.

"Maybe she was busy," Torren said. He sat his empty glass down.

"No. Something is wrong. I can feel it. I'm heading back to Earth."

"Well, since you put it that way, I'm going with you."

"This is my business. You don't have to do this," Eno said.

"Look, I know a man in love when I see him. You're not

going by yourself. You wouldn't be able to think straight anyway."

"What are you talking about?"

"I'm your backup, bud. No arguing."

Eno and Torren headed to the flight deck.

Torren contacted Gadara on his comms. "Gadara, sweetie, I'm helping Eno. It's an emergency. I love you. I'll be back as soon as I can."

"What? You're thinking of going without me?"

"Sorry, babe, it's an emergency. I will return as soon as I can." He turned off his comms.

"That's not good," Eno said.

"Sure it is. She would just argue about going with us."

The two climbed into Transporter One and headed toward Earth.

Mercy, New Mexico

Bear Hunter stood in the center of the office and started a prayer chant.

"What's he doing?" Daniel asked.

"I think he's praying," Sid said.

"Well, I've got to go to the bathroom, so don't do anything until I get back," Daniel said.

Several minutes went by and Sid went to check on Daniel.

"Daniel? Are you okay in there?" Sid asked through the door.

There was no response.

"Daniel?"

Sid tried the door, but it was locked. He pounded on the door, but there was no response. "Damn."

Bear Hunter was behind him. "What's happening?"

"He's not answering and the door is locked."

"Hey, look at this," Bear Hunter pointed to a set of keys stuck in the door of the lady's room.

"What are those—"

Bear Hunter opened the door to the lady's room but it was empty.

"I wonder if the same thing happened to Willow Tree and Yellow Elk?" Bear Hunter said. He handed the keys to Sid.

Sid tried the keys on the men's room door. He tried several of them before one unlocked it. He pushed the door open, but something blocked it. He forced it open. There on the floor was Daniel. It looked like his throat was torn out.

"Shouldn't there be more blood?" Bear Hunter asked.

"Yes. Especially since the carotid artery is missing," Sid said.

"Look!" Bear Hunter pointed to a single track through the blood. It was not human. He glanced around and found a closet in the corner. Bear Hunter went to pull the door open—

"Wait!" Sid had pulled his weapon and stood to the side. He motioned for Bear Hunter to open the door.

There was nothing inside but another single, non-human footprint. Bear Hunter pressed around the back wall of the closet, but found nothing.

"What's this?" Sid pointed to an inconspicuous button on the side of the closet, where a broom hung. He pushed the button and the wall moved away from the closet. He pulled his flashlight off his belt and shined it in a dark cavernous area. There were steps going down. Sid shined the light all around.

"I'll go first," Bear Hunter said.

"Why you?"

"I have a knife." He showed Sid a large knife that could penetrate a body from one end to the other. "If I'm attacked, shoot the damn reptile."

"How do you know it's a reptile?"

"I've seen what they do. And what happened to that man is what they do before eating the person from the inside out."

Bear Hunter slowly and quietly went down the steps. Sid gave him a little head start and went down after him. He continued to shine the light on the steps so they could see where they were going.

Bear Hunter reached the bottom. He sniffed the air. It was a damp, dirt smell. His eyes hadn't adjusted to the dark, so he felt his way along the wall. Most of it was rock, with some dirt. Sid was behind him, shining his flashlight.

Under the stairs was a dead end. The tunnel was wide enough for several people to walk through. Sid's flashlight offered enough light to see there was no one around and no obstacles. They continued following the tunnel until they came to an open area. There were several lit candles tucked in among the rocks, shining on a long, tall table, with a metal crate beneath it.

"This reminds me of an altar," Bear Hunter said.

"I guess we interrupted something," Sid said.

Bear Hunter poked the wall with his knife, up and down and across.

"What are you doing?"

"The entrance to the cave was a hologram. Maybe there is a hologram here." Sid joined him with the flashlight.

Finally, the knife went through air. Bear Hunter stepped in and Sid was behind him. It was a small area, bigger than the closet, but not much. They faced a ladder in the wall. Bear Hunter went up first. When he reached the top, there was something wooden overhead. He pushed up on it, looking through a crack. He was floor level in an office. He was looking at the backside of a desk and chair. He pushed the floor up higher and crawled out. Sid came up after him.

"We're in the Chief's office!" he said.

Bear Hunter glanced around. "There's another footprint," he said. He followed it out.

"He's one step ahead of us," Sid said.

Bear Hunter went back to the bathrooms to check the women's side. There was no door or hologram. He went back to the men's bathroom. Daniel was still there, on the floor, but there was no hologram or any other secret doors.

Sid called someone on the phone. "We're going to need backup."

"Do all your officers have portables that they take home, along with chargers?" Bear Hunter asked.

"Yes, we do. Why?"

"Maybe someone knew where Willow Tree would be."

"What are you getting at?"

"Even when Willow Tree is off, she sometimes leaves the radio on in case the officer needs help, so she could back them up."

"You think one of our officers shifted into a reptile?"

"Maybe. Who have you not accounted for?"

"Well, Willow Tree couldn't get a list of those arrested. We know the Chief and mayor are dead." Sid rubbed his chin. "None of us have been able to reach Carmela or Darryl. Do you think one of them is doing this?"

"If they are really reptilian, yes. I know the Chief and the mayor came to my house. They shifted before my eyes into reptilians and then shifted again into me and Yellow Elk."

"So, if the Chief is reptilian, then Carmela is too."

"Who did you call?" Bear Hunter asked.

"I called Kyle. He's coming in."

"Don't use your radio. Otherwise, the other person would know what you're doing."

"Well, Carmela didn't take a radio home, but Darryl did," Sid said.

"So maybe Darryl is your suspect," Bear Hunter said.

Sid texted Kyle to not use the radio. Then he texted all the others to come in.

"When they get here, we need to go back to the tunnel and check again for more holograms. We've got to find Yellow Elk and Willow Tree," Bear Hunter said.

"I need to get an ambulance here for Daniel," Sid said.

"I think it's too late for that."

"You're right." Sid picked up the phone and called the county coroner.

By the time Kyle and David showed up, the coroner arrived. Sid led him to the body and the coroner and his team started working on Daniel.

"He was so good at dispatching," Kyle said.

"Yeah, for a newbie, he sure was good."

Carl and Ed showed up. Sid filled everyone in on what was happening. They waited for the coroner's team to wrap things up and take Daniel's body.

"We're going to take another look down there and make sure there are no bodies. Other than that, I don't know where to look," Sid said.

"I'm going with you," Bear Hunter said.

"Okay, someone needs to stay up here. Lock the doors," Sid said.

No one volunteered.

"If it's Darryl, he's got a key," Carl said.

"If someone doesn't stay up here, he could lock us all in the tunnel." Sid shoved his hands on his hips. "All right! I'll stay. You all be careful." He handed his flashlight to Bear Hunter.

The group started with the stairs from the bathroom entrance.

"How long has this been here?" Kyle asked.

"I've been here the longest, and I never knew about it," Carl said.

By the time they reached the bottom, Bear Hunter gave instructions. "Feel along the walls. If there's a hologram, your hand will go through it. Holler when you find it and use your flashlights."

"Hey, I found something here," Ed said. He pulled his gun out with one hand and his flashlight in the other. It was the dead end behind the stairs.

"I'll go with you," Carl said. He did the same with his gun and flashlight.

David, Kyle, and Bear Hunter continued on. There were no other holograms leading up to the altar area.

"What's in the crate?" Kyle asked.

"We didn't check it," Bear Hunter said.

The three of them pulled it out from under the table.

Eno and Torren hovered over the parking lot of the Police Station.

"There's Willow Tree's car!" Eno said.

"How do you know? It looks like they're all here," Torren said.

"Her number is on the side. They're each numbered."

"Got it. Are we going to land?"

"Yes." Eno set the ship down several yards away, behind the station, near an abandoned old building along the side road.

"Leave the cloaking on," Torren said.

"Good idea."

Eno pulled out his favorite weapon, but before he opened the ramp, Torren stopped him.

"There's a damn reptile," Torren said.

The reptile sneaked from some brush behind the abandoned building to the front.

Torren grabbed his new weapon as well and nodded.

Eno let the ramp down.

The two of them practically ran to the building and when the creature saw them, he pulled the door open. Torren was a little quicker on the draw and evaporated the creature. Eno evaporated the door. Something fell to the ground.

Eno picked up the radio the creature dropped.

"He's one of them!" Eno said.

"One of who?"

"A police officer!"

Eno tried once more to contact Willow Tree. '*Willow Tree, I love you now and forever.*'

Torren waited. "Anything?"

"No."

"Does she still have her comms on?"

"Yes! Willow Tree, come in, this is Eno. Can you read?"

No response.

"God, I hope she's all right," Torren said.

"Me, too."

A crackling sounded, then, "Willow Tree, come in, this is Eno. Can you read?"

"Oh my God!" Bear Hunter said. "They're in this crate."

The three of them tried to open it, but it was nailed down.

Bear Hunter used his knife to pry it open, but it wasn't strong enough.

"We need a crow bar," Kyle said.

"If we could only get this up that ladder," David said.

"It's too heavy, even for the three of us," Bear Hunter said.

"Hey, look what we found," Carl said.

Carl and Ed came through the hologram with Eno and Torren. Bear Hunter stood and glanced past the altar, catching a glimpse of his future son-in-law.

"Just in time, Eno. We heard your communicator go off, so we knew Willow Tree is in this crate. I only hope Yellow Elk is with her."

"Stand back," Eno ordered. "Put your weapon on half power, Torren, and only aim at the lid."

Torren got on the opposite side of the crate.

"On my count, one, two, three." He shot the edge of the top and so did his best friend. It melted away.

Both women were inside, bound and gagged.

"We'll take them up the stairs," Eno said. He picked up Willow Tree and Torren picked up Yellow Elk. Once they were upstairs, they took them through to the break room and lay them on the floor.

Bear Hunter was right behind them with their weapons and handed Eno the knife. Eno quickly cut the ropes around

Willow Tree's hands and feet and handed the knife back to Bear Hunter.

By the time Bear Hunter had cut Yellow Elk free, Eno had carefully pulled the tape away from Willow Tree's mouth and pulled out the cloth that was inside her mouth. He hugged her to him. Bear Hunter did the same with Yellow Elk.

"I only wish we had a healer with us," Eno said.

"Willow Tree is a healer," Bear Hunter said.

There was a commotion in the other room. Eno realized there were a lot of men surrounding them, wearing the same police uniform.

"We all came when Sid said something's happened to Willow Tree," Kyle said.

"Thank you. That means a lot to me," Eno said.

"Yeah, well, now she's our new Chief. Can't let anything happen to her, you know," David said.

"Your new Chief of Police?" Eno asked.

"Hey, a promotion. That's great news!" Torren said.

"Did I hear someone ask for a healer?" Genesis said, barging into the room. Gadara stood beside her with her hands on her hips.

"Torren Conley, don't ever do that again! I'm the only backup you need. You got that!"

He saluted her. "Yes, Captain." He glanced at the men in the room. "I love it when she does that." They all chuckled.

Genesis began her healing chant over both women. Then she concentrated over Willow Tree and moved on to Yellow Elk.

She checked their eyes. "I believe these two have been drugged. We need to get them to the Med Beds as soon as possible." Adam brought in a hover gurney and Keely followed him with another.

"Did you bring the whole team, Captain Gadara?" Eno asked.

"Of course. When a friend is in need, we go together."

Several of the men in the room helped lift Willow Tree onto the gurney and then did the same for Yellow Elk.

"We'll be back when they are completely healed," Eno said.

"We'll notify the military about this tunnel. They will come and destroy it like they did the others," Captain Tremol said.

"So, Carl, you're the assistant Chief, what happens now?" Sid asked.

"We go home and pretend this never happened?" Kyle said.

"No, we pick up extra shifts, that's what we do." Carl pulled the schedule off the bulletin board and started making changes.

Bear Hunter followed the Vaedran team to the door. "Thank you, boys, for saving my family," he said.

They all did a thumbs up and went back to the schedule.

Bear Hunter flew back to the Concordance with Eno, since Torren went back with Gadara and the other crew on Transporter Two.

"I never told the others," Eno said.

"Told them what?" Bear Hunter asked.

"I never told them I asked Willow Tree to be my mate."

Bear Hunter patted him on the back. "It's okay. I'm sure they will be happy for you."

"But, now that's she's Chief, will she want to leave that job, for me?"

"She loves you. Willow Tree will go where you go."

"I've been thinking about our future. Me and Willow Tree," Eno said. "When I'm finished teaching the pilots here, I will return to the Star Force. I'm not sure if I will still be on the Concordance, or another ship. I've got six years left of my service. Willow Tree will either have to stay here or stay on Chroma until I return."

"You don't get to take leave?"

Eno glanced at him, his brows raised.

"You know, time off. A vacation?"

"Oh, yes, time off. We get that once an ano for about two weeks."

"That is a long time to be away from your loved ones."

"That's why so many in the military are single. We don't even think about looking for mates until we get out."

"What about the Admiral?"

"What do you mean?"

"How did he deal with it when you were younger?"

"There was a time when I was on his ship with him and my mother. I was real young then. And after, when I was a teenager, I was with him. Then there was a time I was with my mother on another ship. She was with the Star Force as well. They weren't always stationed on the same ship."

"Well, there you go," Bear Hunter said.

"What do you mean?"

"There's a way for it to work out. Ask your father. He will know."

By the time they reached the Concordance, Willow Tree and Yellow Elk were already in the Med Beds. Eno and Bear Hunter kept vigil outside the room until Conn showed up.

"Eno, great news," she said.

"What is it?" He stood at her approach.

"We discovered what the drug was and we were able to diffuse it. We are clearing it out of their bodies as we speak."

"How much longer?"

"Maybe thirty minutes. I will let you know." Conn bowed, then left.

After a few minutes, all his friends showed up.

"Are they awake yet?" Genesis asked.

"Not yet," Eno said.

Captain Gadara and Torren stood next to him, Captain Tremol and Keely were in the middle, and Adam and Genesis were on the end.

"I need to tell you all something," Eno said.

"What is it?" Torren asked.

"I've asked Willow Tree to be my mate."

"Awesome!" Adam smacked his arm. "Congratulations!"

Captain Tremol hit the nail on the head. "Why aren't you happy, then?"

"I don't know if we can be together," Eno said.

"If his father made it work, Eno can make it work, too," Bear Hunter said.

"There's only one way to find out," Captain Gadara said. "Admiral Esrith, this is Captain Gadara. Your presence is needed in the Med Center, Gadara out." She glanced at her chrono.

"Why did you do that?"

"Because you look depressed and you need an answer now," she said.

It was a few moments until Admiral Esrith showed up. "What's happened? Who's hurt?" Esrith said, walking into the area.

Captain Gadara pointed to Eno.

"Eno? Are you all right?" Admiral Esrith touched his arm, making Eno look up.

Eno scratched his head. "Physically, I'm fine."

"Get on with it," Torren said.

"I've asked Willow Tree to be my mate."

The Admiral cocked his head at Eno, then glanced at everyone else. "That sounded like good news coming from someone who doesn't seem happy about it."

"I love her, but I don't know how we can be together."

"What? Is that what you are worried about?"

"Yes, sir. I don't remember us being together as a family that much when I was in my teens."

"You don't? Well, we were all together until you were ten anos. Your mother's ambition was to be an admiral. You can't have two admirals on one ship. You recall when she transferred to another ship? She did that to earn her stripes. Remember that she took you with her for a few anos, then I had you for a few anos? We did that so she could make admiral. By then, you were old enough to join the Star Force. She's currently the admiral of the Ninevah. We spend all our leave time together, but we take it at different times to make it last longer."

"Are you saying we can be together on this ship? While I'm in the Star Force?"

"You're forgetting you will be training pilots on Earth for a time. When you are through, you will go back on whatever ship is in this area. Besides, if Willow Tree doesn't have military aspirations, she will be with you always."

"Yes, we will still be bringing people to Earth and back to Vaedra for a while, Eno," Keely said.

"There's always work on a ship that she can pick up to keep from being bored," Admiral Esrith said.

"In that case, you're all invited to the mating ceremony," Eno said.

"That's the Eno I know," Torren said.

Esrith gave Eno a hug. "Congratulations, son. I'm truly happy for you."

"I'm truly happy, too."

"Excuse, please. Happy day! Willow Tree and Yellow Elk are awake," Conn said.

Eno and Bear Hunter rushed into the room. Both women were sitting up, the Med Bed chambers opened.

Eno scooped Willow Tree into his arms. He kissed her tenderly on the mouth. She reached her arms around him and pulled him into a more passionate kiss.

Bear Hunter kissed Yellow Elk as if he hadn't seen her in a long time.

The group of people cheered.

"What's happening?" Willow Tree asked.

"My friends are now your friends," he said.

"I guess that means more people are coming for the ceremony?"

"Yep."

"Eno, before Daryl drugged us, he said those parents were compensated for those children." She touched his cheek.

"What?" Eno's eyes widened.

"Yes, those parents didn't want their children. The children were paid for and the parents were told to leave town. That's why we couldn't find them."

"That's disgusting," Adam said. "They sold their kids like pieces of meat."

"They need to be in Gitmo along with the pedophiles," Keely said.

Two days later, on the Mescalero Apache Indian Reservation, all of Willow Tree's family was there and all of Eno's friends and family were there. They had gathered under a thatched roof pavilion. Eno was dressed in a white dress shirt and white jeans and wrapped in a blue blanket. Willow Tree stood next to him in a white, knee-length sundress and also wrapped in a blue blanket. Her long hair hung past her butt with two thin braids going down each side of her face with tiny white flowers woven in. Both of them wore white moccasins.

The medicine man, who happened to be an ordained minister, stood before them. He spoke in Apache and chanted a prayer, blessing them with sacred cattail pollen.

Then Torren took Eno's blanket and Gadara took Willow Tree's blanket. Yellow Elk walked up to them and wrapped a white blanket around both of them.

"Now you will feel no rain for each of you will be shelter to the other. Now you will feel no cold, for each of you will be warmth for the other. Go now to your dwelling place to enter into the days of your togetherness and may your days be good and long upon the Earth."

The medicine man thanked everyone and blessed the tribe.

After he left, four Apache Gaan dancers performed for Eno and Willow Tree, while the women prepared a table with food and refreshments. When the dance was over, everyone flocked to the table.

"There's a lot more to this ceremony, but I wanted to keep it simple," Willow Tree said.

"Simple is good. I like simple," Eno said.

Willow Tree took Eno around to meet his new family, while Bear Hunter and Yellow Elk kept Admiral Esrith company, introducing him to other family and friends.

By the time Eno met everyone, it was time to see her new friends from the Concordance.

Yellow Elk came up to her with a small, wrapped gift.

"I almost forgot. Thank you, Mom." She took the gift from her mother and handed it to Eno. "This is for you, my love."

He unwrapped the gift and inside was a photo of the two of them she had taken with her phone.

"I love it." He kissed her tenderly.

"There will be plenty more pictures after today," she said. She pointed to the photographer her mother had hired.

He held the photo to his heart. "I love this photo of us and this blanket," Eno said.

"My mother made it for me years ago for when I married."

"Well, we sleep under this tonight." He pulled her close and kissed her again.

"Uh, Eno?"

"Yes, my Willow Tree?"

"Where are we sleeping tonight?"

He raised his brows.

Bear Hunter walked up to them. "Here," he said. He handed Eno an envelope. "I got you two a room at the Hilton in Las Cruces."

"Thanks, Dad," Willow Tree said.

"Yeah, thanks Dad." Eno shook his hand.

After spending time speaking with everyone there and moving throughout the gathering, the two of them slipped off into Willow Tree's VW Bug and drove off into the sunset.

End

REDEMPTION

The Vaedra Chronicles Series
Book One in the Vaedra Saga

Dram aimed the robotic powered plasma drill at the target and squeezed the handles. In a matter of minutes, liquid tulin poured into the wheeled vat below the hole. When it reached the fill line, he had the next vat lined up.

"Vat's up!" he yelled. He pushed the full vat down the track and concentrated on filling the new vat.

Gomet grabbed the vat and pushed it to the next link, where the tulin would be poured into the grand vat. From there, it would be made into coins or bars or melted into exquisite furniture.

He remembered when he owned furniture made of tulin and spent the coins on ships to increase his business.

He lined up the plasma drill once more when the flow of

tulin stopped. Pressing the handles, he tried to get more tulin to pour out, but this vein was done. He reached up and pulled the sensor down to locate more of the shiny gold-colored metal.

Moving the sensor around, up and down the rock wall, it finally beeped. He marked the spot and moved his vat into place and began the same routine. More liquid tulin flowed after the plasma drill did its thing.

He couldn't imagine doing this kind of work without these tools. The only reason humans were needed was to move the vats along and to manually use the sensor. Oh, and the fact that it was punishment for living a life of crime. Yeah, that's the reason.

"I heard we were getting another cell-mate," Gomet said.

"Did you, now?" He pushed the filled vat to Gomet.

He walked back a ways to pick up another empty vat and push it along to his target area. He could only get so much out of a vein with one blast.

"So, when is this new cell-mate coming in?" he asked. He aimed his plasma drill again and blasted another vein of tulin.

He watched the liquid pour into the vat.

"Tonight," Gomet said.

"Hmmm." Gomet usually got good intel. A new cellmate didn't come along too often. It would be amusing for a while, but then he would get bored harassing the newbie. But cell-mates didn't mean they would be working together. They would just be sleeping in the same cell. Right now, it was him, Gomet, and Thadus. After this newbie, there were no more beds.

Thadus worked the gem mines. The work was harder, but not as hot. Here, in the tulin mines, the high heat to melt the tulin into coins, bars, or furnishings kept the whole place sweltering. His tank top was grimy and worn and so were his pants. Once every six months, they were given some clean, recycled clothes and the old ones were washed and passed along to someone else.

Thadus used his chisel to work the rubies out of their rock enclosure. He had an eye for detail, and this was slow, tedious work. The more he was able to pry the bigger rubies out, the bigger his bonus at the end of the month.

He hung from his harness over a wall of sparkling rubies. Besides himself, there were two others who could dislodge the beauties in big pieces. They all wanted that bonus. He was planning on buying a pillow with his earnings. The flattened pillow he had was giving him neck pains and he dreamed of a good night's sleep.

Once a month, when the bonuses were given out, they had a small market set up where the prisoners could buy things they needed or wanted, luxury items that normal people took for granted.

"Thadus!"

He turned to see who called him. That was odd because no one ever called him. He caught a glimpse of movement below him on a ledge.

"Coming up!" a voice called out.

Within seconds, a woman was hoisted up next to him in a harness. Her hair was black with orange spikes coming out from it, reminding him of a matchstick.

"I'm Tam," she said.

"Well, I'm Thadus. I guess you're the newbie I heard talk about."

"I guess so."

"Let me show you what I'm doing and then you can attack that wall over there."

He reached above her head and pulled her rope closer to his. He showed her how to hold the chisel and the mallet, then went to work.

"It's simple really. If you take your time and do it right, you get a bonus each month for the big rubies. If you break them, you get nothing."

"I didn't think prisoners got paid at all," she said.

"We don't. The bonus helps to buy things like a blanket or pillow or clothes. Just a little something to make our hell on Plumaris a little easier to bear."

Thadus reached up to the rope above her harness, and shoved

Tam further away.

"That's the end of your lesson. You're on your own now."

"Thanks," she mumbled.

Thadus went back to work. Each ruby he extracted was carefully placed into a bag he had on his waist.

"Where's my bag?" Tam asked.

"Didn't they give you one?"

"Nope."

Thadus patted his grimy clothes and found a spare bag. He pushed off from the rock wall and slid sideways to reach Tam.

"Here. You should have gotten one when they hooked you up to the harness."

"I guess they overlooked that part," she said.

Hours later, an alarm sounded, and the harnesses were lowered to the ground.

"What's happening?" Tam asked.

"It's quitting time," Thadus said.

A guard unhooked each of them from their harness and pointed to a wall with a box protruding out from it.

"Deposit your rubies with your code over there," the guard said.

"What code?" Tam asked.

"Weren't you given a code when they processed you?"

"I don't remember a code."

"Name?"

"Tam."

"Your code is 043," the guard said. He glanced at his comm-pad. "Don't forget that number. You need it for everything."

"Yes, sir." Tam walked to the box and pressed her code into the keypad beside it and it opened. She deposited her rubies inside the box and the box closed.

"Now what?" she said.

"You go to your cell," the guard said.

"She's a newbie," Thadus said. "I don't think she has been assigned a cell yet."

"Wait there," the guard said. He pointed to a spot against the wall.

After Thadus and two others deposited their rubies and went on, the guard approached her.

"Come with me," he said.

"Is this our daily routine, then?" Tam asked.

"You came late today. Tomorrow, you eat breakfast and put in ten hours with two breaks and a lunch then go back to your cell at the end of the day."

"Sounds like fun." Tam said, sarcastically.

The guard gave her a side glance.

They walked through the tunnel before getting into a people

mover. After a few minutes, the people mover stopped, and they

exited.

"This is your cell block." The guard checked his comm-pad again. "This way." He turned right and she followed him down a hall. It looked more like a building than a cave. Each cell appeared to have four men in them. There were cells on each side of the hall. The guard stopped at the last one on the right and unlocked the cell.

There was Thadus, along with two others.

"There must be some mistake," she said.

"No. This is your cell."

"Where are the women's cells?"

"You're the first, so there aren't any," the guard said.

All three men stood frozen, glancing at each other, then her, then the guard.

"You've got to be kidding," a tall Chromian said.

"Enjoy the company, boys." The guard shoved her inside and closed the cell.

"Hello, Tam," Thadus said.

Now that she could actually see, she realized he was Caucasian and so was the other man. All three were a bit grimy and...old.

Her stomach growled, reminding her she hadn't eaten all day. She hoped there was a meal tonight.

"There's your bed," the Chromian said. He pointed to the

bunk on top. It had a mattress, but that was all. No sheets, no pillow.

"Thanks," she said. She climbed up the side to get to her bunk. She was tired. But then, she remembered she had to pee. She climbed back down.

"Where's the toilet?"

All three men stepped aside, and she could see it, out in the open, with a sink beside it.

Great. No privacy. And no shower. Well, she had to go and there wasn't anything she could do about it. She just pretended they weren't there and did her business. Maybe it would get easier. But when she finished, she realized, they had all turned their backs to her. Hmm. Is this what they did for each other, too?

Before she could climb up to the top bunk, the Chromian grabbed her arm.

"What are you doing here? You're just a kid."

"I'm older than I look, old man."

"Old man?" Thadus asked.

The other Caucasian laughed.

"I asked you a question," the Chromian said.

She glanced at his hand, still holding her arm, then glared into his eyes.

"I poisoned a man, sabotaged a couple ships, and tried to kill another man, is that okay with you?"

"Did you say you sabotaged a couple ships?" Thadus asked.

"That's right." The Chromian pulled her toward him as the other two gathered around.

"I remember you. You're the one that helped us find that traitor, Berto."

"Yes. You were with the pirates that boarded the ship we were on."

"Berto? The man with telekinetic powers?" The Chromian asked.

"That's the one," she said.

"How do you know Berto?" Thadus asked the Chromian.

"He worked for me," the Chromian said.

"Well, it looks like we all have something in common, don't we?" She said.

The Chromian turned her loose. She looked him over. For an old man, he had a nice body, which was more than she could say for the other two.

"How do you know Berto?" The Chromian asked her.

"He killed my brother."

ABOUT THE AUTHOR

Ester López is a writer and publisher and lives in the Smoky Mountains, where she has been writing sci-fi and paranormal adventure romances for almost 30 years. To keep up to date on Ester's book releases and book signings, please join her Readers Group at www.esterlopez.com.
Follow Ester's Blogs at
www.esterlopez.com
www.AuthorBlogSpot.esterlopez.com
To Purchase Ester's signed books, go to her publisher's website at www.writingphotographicservicesllc.com